从经典作家进入历史

希尼朗诵《瀑布》，一九六六年。（北爱尔兰数字电影档案）

希尼出生于北爱尔兰德里郡。他的第一本诗集
《一个博物学家之死》初版于一九六六年，后
又出版了诗歌、批评和翻译作品，使他成为他
那一代诗人中的翘楚。一九九五年，他获得诺
贝尔文学奖；两度荣获惠特布莱德年度图书奖
（《酒精水准仪》，1996；《贝奥武甫》，1999）。
由丹尼斯·奥德里斯科尔主持的访谈录《踏脚
石》出版于二〇〇八年；他的最后一本诗集《人
之链》获得二〇一〇年度前瞻诗歌奖最佳诗集
奖。二〇一三年，希尼去世。他翻译的维吉尔
《埃涅阿斯纪》第六卷在其去世后出版（2016），
赢得批评界盛誉。

◇中英双语版◇

一个博物学家之死

进入黑暗之门

[爱尔兰] 谢默斯·希尼 著　朱玉 译

广西师范大学出版社
·桂林·

一个博物学家之死

1966

给玛丽

目录

致　谢

　　一些诗曾发表在以下书刊上，谨向这些书刊的编辑致谢：

　　《贝尔法斯特电讯报》、《都柏林杂志》、《基尔肯尼杂志》、《趣味》、《爱尔兰时报》、《倾听者》、《新政治家》、《北方评论》、《前哨》、《爱尔兰诗歌》、《时尚》、《阿尔斯特艺术》(BBC 北爱尔兰)、《当代诗人》和《诗人之声》(BBC 三台节目)、《大学诗歌 5》、《一九六五年度英联邦青年诗人作品选》(海涅曼)。

挖　掘

在我的食指与拇指之间
短粗的笔卧着；安稳如枪。

在我窗下，清晰刺耳的声响
是铁锹陷入粗砺的土壤：
我父亲，挖掘。我往下看

直到他绷紧的臀部在花圃间
蹲下，又起身，恍若二十年前
土豆垄里有节奏的俯身
那是他在挖掘。

粗朴的靴子依偎着铁锹，手柄
牢牢抵住膝盖内侧掘动。
他拔起高高的茎叶，把光亮的锹刃深埋
土中翻起新土豆，我们拾起来，
喜欢它们在我们掌中冰凉的坚硬。

天啊，老父还能使唤铁锹。
就像他的老父亲。

我爷爷一天割下的泥炭
比托纳沼泽上的任何人都多。
一次我给他送去一瓶牛奶，
瓶口用纸随意塞着。他直身
饮下，又立刻开始干活

利落地切切割割，把草皮
抛过肩后，不断向深处
寻找好泥炭。挖掘。

土豆霉的清冷气味，湿泥炭
吱吱嘎嘎的声音，快刀切穿
鲜活的根茎，在我脑海苏醒。
但我没有铁锹去追随他们。

在我的食指与拇指之间
短粗的笔卧着。
我将用它挖掘。

一个博物学家之死

一整年亚麻池在小镇中心
化脓；碧绿且头脑昏沉的
亚麻已腐烂，被巨大的草皮压弯。
每天它都热晕在惩罚的烈日中。
气泡轻声咕哝，绿头蝇
环绕臭味织出嘹亮的音幔。
还有蜻蜓，还有斑点蝶，
但都不如那温热浓稠的黏液，
是蛙卵在池岸阴凉处生长
如凝结的水。在这里，每年春天，
我都用果酱罐装满果冻般的
卵粒，排列在家中的窗台，
学校的搁架，等待并观察直到
不断发胖的卵爆裂，成为灵敏
游动的蝌蚪。沃尔斯小姐告诉我们
蛙爸爸为何称为牛蛙，
它怎么呱呱叫，蛙妈妈怎么
产出成百上千个小小的蛋，也就是
蛙卵。你还可以根据青蛙来判断天气，

因为晴天它们是黄色，雨天

是棕色。

　　然后在炎热的一天当田野散发

草丛里牛粪的臭味，愤怒的蛙群

侵略了亚麻池；我躲进树篱，

听到一阵从未听过的沙哑

蛙鸣。空气里充满低音部的合唱。

就在那池塘，大肚囊的青蛙在草皮上

拨动扳机，松垮的脖子鼓动如帆。有的跃起：

噼噼啪啪发出丑陋的威胁。有的坐着，

姿态如泥制的榴弹，扁平的脑袋在放屁。

我恶心，转身，逃跑。黏液之王

在那里集结伺机复仇，而我知道，

假如我伸出手就会被蛙卵抓住。

谷 仓

筛好的谷粒堆积如象牙颗粒
或如双耳袋中坚实的水泥。
霉味的黑暗贮藏着一批军火
内有农具、马具和铧犁。

地板是鼠灰、平滑、冰冷的混凝土。
没有窗户，只有两束狭长的光映射
镀金微尘，交错，从每一处
山墙顶端的通风孔射入。唯一的门意味着

整个夏天都不通风，当锌板滚烫如火炉。
镰刀的利刃，洁净的铁锹，干草叉的尖齿：
当你走进去，光亮的物件缓缓显露。
然后你感到蛛网把你的双肺阻滞

于是迅速逃入阳光照耀的庭院——
逃入夜晚，当蝙蝠们翩翩飞行
在睡之椽的上空，明亮的双眼
从角落的谷堆里盯视，凶猛，目不转睛。

黑暗吞噬如屋顶下的空间。我是谷壳
等待从通风孔飞进来的鸟儿啄食。
我面朝下趴着，躲避上方的恐吓。
双耳袋移动如瞎眼的硕鼠。

学问的进阶

我选择走河堤

（一如既往，避免

桥梁）。河流小心翼翼，

柔顺，油光，映现

山墙和天空的图案。

我俯身倚靠栏杆，

现已远离公路，

打量脏脊背的天鹅。

什么在吐口水，那么粗鲁，那么近，

污染这寂静：一只大老鼠

黏糊糊地钻出水面，

我的喉咙立刻恶心想吐

于是我一身冷汗往回走，

但是天啊，但见另一只

敏捷上岸，在石上遗留

它潮湿的弧线。难以置信，

我竟建起一片可怕的
桥头阵地。我转过身，
以从容、兴奋的审慎
瞪视曾被我怠慢的啮齿动物。

它茫然而机械地摆了摆，
停下来，弓起背，亮晶晶，
耳朵紧贴它圆滚滚的脑袋
潜伏在那里偷听。

它身后那条渐细的尾巴，
雨滴的眼睛，古老的口鼻：
一个个我全都接纳。
它瞄准我。我瞪着它

忘记了我曾经多么恐慌
当它的灰兄弟们抓挠和吃饭
在我们院里的鸡笼后方，
在我床铺上面的天花板。

这恐怖的家伙，冰冷，湿毛，小爪，
沿着一根污水管道逃亡。
我在它背后瞪了一分钟。
然后我继续赶路，跨过桥梁。

摘黑莓

给菲利普·霍布斯鲍姆①

八月底，只要大雨和阳光

持续一星期，黑莓就会熟。

起初，只一颗，光亮瘀紫的一团

在其他红的、青的硬结之间。

你吃下那最初的一颗，果肉甘美

如浓郁的葡萄酒：夏天的血液在里面，

给舌头留下颜色和采摘

的欲念。然后红果呈墨色，那种饥渴

让我们带着牛奶罐、豌豆罐和果酱罐外出，

灌木划破皮肤，湿草漂洗靴子。

在牧草田、小麦田和土豆垄周边

我们跋涉并采摘直到罐子装满，

直到叮当作响的罐底铺好

青涩果实，而上方团团大墨滴燃烧

如一盘眼睛。我们的手上都是刺，

我们的掌心有黏血，如同蓝胡子。

---

① 菲利普·霍布斯鲍姆（Philip Hobsbaum，1932-2005），英国诗人。曾任职于贝尔法斯特女王大学，成立"贝尔法斯特小组"，促进了当地诗人间的交流。年轻的希尼曾应邀加入，对其创作产生重要影响。（此类脚注为译者注，下同，不另标出）

我们把新鲜的浆果贮藏在牛棚。

但浴缸装满时我们发现一层毛绒，

鼠灰色的霉菌，饱食我们的秘藏。

果汁也变臭了。一旦离开树枝，

果实就会发酵，甜果肉变酸。

我总是想哭。这不公平，

所有可爱的罐子都散发腐味。

年年我都希望它们保存，明知它们不会。

搅乳日

一层厚皮，纹理粗糙如石灰毛坯，

在四个陶缸的表面渐渐变硬，

陶缸，如陶制大炸弹，立在小小的食物间。

在奶牛腺体、反刍食物和乳房的热酿之后，

凉爽透气的陶器发酵脱脂乳，

迎接搅乳日，这一天箍紧的搅拌桶会被

滚开的热水壶清洗，忙碌的刷子

在风干的木材上发出美味的回音。

洗净后，它便立在厨房的石板地上。

接着摆出四陶缸，宽厚的唇边泻出

奶油，它们白色的内脏，流入消过毒的搅拌桶。

柱塞，如松木制成的巨型威士忌

搅拌棒，猛然插入，盖子闭合。

我妈妈第一个搅拌，定下节奏，

连续几小时砰砰作响。手臂酸痛。

手掌起泡。面庞和衣裳都溅满

松软的乳汁。

        金色的斑点终于

开始飞舞。于是他们倒入热水，

消毒一个桦木碗

和几把波纹小黄油铲。

他们短促的搅拌加快，突然，

一层黄色凝乳压着翻滚的白乳，

厚重醇浓，凝固的阳光，

他们捞起，滴淌，在阔口锡滤器中，

然后堆在碗里如镀金的沙砾。

搅乳日过后房子会臭很久，

刺鼻如硫矿。那些空陶缸

重新沿着墙边排列，黄油

垫着软印花板堆在食品架上。

房间里我们充实而轻松地走动。

大脑也结晶，满脑都是洁净的松木搅乳器，

酸牛奶的泼溅声和汩汩声，

小铲在湿黄油块上的拍打声。

早年的肃清

六岁时我第一次看到小猫溺亡。
丹·塔格特把它们，"皮包骨的小崽子"，
抛进水桶；微弱的金属声响，

柔软的小爪抓狂。但它们细小的喧嚣
很快被浸泡。它们被吊在
水泵的出水口，水流滔滔。

"它们现在岂不是更好？"丹说。
小猫像湿手套浮动闪烁直到
被抛进粪堆，光滑地死了。

突如其来的恐惧，一连几天我在庭院
悲伤徘徊，看着三个浸水的残骸
变得斑白脆弱如夏日陈积的粪便

直到我忘了它们。但恐惧重返
当丹抓大老鼠，捕野兔，射乌鸦
或拉扯老母鸡的脖子，令人憎厌。

然而，生活取代了虚情假意，

如今，当尖叫的幼崽被拎去溺毙，

我不过耸耸肩，"该死的崽子"。这一切合理：

"阻止虐杀"的谈论在城里可行

那里的人们认为死亡残酷，

但在管理得当的农场，有害物必须被肃清。

跟随者

我父亲用马拉犁劳动，
他的双肩隆起如满帆
挂在犁柄与田埂当中。
马儿在他的口令下苦干。

一位行家。他装好犁翼，
安上光亮的钢尖犁铧。
泥土便开始翻滚不息。
在垄头，他只消一拉

缰绳，流汗的马儿便
转回田中。他的眼睛
眯起，斜睨着地面，
精准地丈量田埂。

我在他靴钉的足印里跌撞，
有时也摔倒在光滑的草泥上；
有时，他把我背在身后，
随着他沉重的步伐升降。

我想要长大、耕耘，

闭上一只眼，绷紧臂弯。

但我所做的只是跟随

他宽大的影子漫步田间。

我曾是个讨厌鬼，跌跌，绊绊，

喋喋不休。但如今

是我父亲一直步履蹒跚

跟在我身后，不离不弃。

祖先像

下巴像萝卜般膨胀圆滚，
双目无神似雕像，上唇
压迫厚重的嘴巴向下垂凹。
圆礼帽令人想起爱尔兰演员
一半面无表情，一半傲慢。
银表链绕在他身上如圈套。

我父亲的叔叔，曾教父亲干活，
长期定格于褐色影像，现已褪色
必须取下。如今卧室墙上
他曾在的地方留下褪色的补丁——
如同皮肤撕下绷带后的情形——
空白的饰板见证家族的兴亡。

二十年前我曾帮忙放牛
把它们赶进圈里或靠着墙头
直到我父亲最终胜利
与一群买牛的人讨价还价，
他们拍牛屁，抓乳头，站住，停下，
然后买来酒水敲定交易。

叔叔和侄儿，五十年前，
也曾在赶集的日子放牧叫喊。
相框里这酒桶身材的家伙：
我看见他把时髦的帽子推向脑后，
拇指伸出马甲，干脆地拍手
卖货。父亲，我看见你也这样做，

看见你黯然神伤，当集市被关停。
商贩将失去立足之地如果农民
都像家庭主妇在拍卖场采购。
你的手杖依然在门后停放。
合上我们编年史的这一章，
我把你叔叔的肖像拿上阁楼。

期中休假

整个上午我坐在校医务室，
点数铃声如丧钟宣告课终。
两点钟，邻居们开车载我回家。

在门廊我遇见哭泣的父亲——
他一向从容应付丧事——
大个子吉姆·埃文斯说这是沉重的打击。

我进门时，婴儿咕咕叫咯咯笑
晃动婴儿车，而我感到窘迫
见到老人们起身和我握手

告诉我他们"为我的不幸难过"。
耳语向陌生人通报我是长子，
在外读书，母亲把我的手握在

她手中并咳出愤怒无泪的叹息。
十点钟时救护车抵达，
载着被护士们止血包好的遗体。

第二天早上我走进房间。雪花莲

和烛光慰藉床边；六周来

我第一次看见他。如今更苍白，

左太阳穴有一块罂粟花般的瘀血，

他躺在四英尺的盒子中如卧婴儿床。

没有刺眼的伤痕，保险杠把他撞飞。

四英尺的盒子，一英尺是一岁。

黎明狩猎

云搅拌它们潮湿的灰浆，把破晓涂成
灰色。石子发出嘲笑的咔嗒
若我们踩空枕木；但大多时候
我们沉默地沿着铁轨走，
那里唯一的蒸汽正袅袅升起，
来自树篱那一边蹲伏的奶牛，
它们反刍，观望，了知。
铁轨成功击中桥洞的
靶心。长脚秧鸡盘问，
出人意料如鲁莽的哨兵，
沙锥鸟以火箭之速升空侦察。
脚踩胶靴，荷枪实弹，利落如伞兵，
我们俩爬上铁门并纵身跃入
草原上六英亩的金雀花、荆豆花和露水中。

一座沙堤，被盘根错节所巩固，
面向你，在铁轨两百码开外。
我们舒服地趴在枯萎的荆豆坡上，
饥饿的眼睛逐渐适应灰暗，
安顿下来，很快就挖好了陷阱。

这就是它们现在都将前往的窝，

阔步走在干水渠的蕨草下，扑闪

棕色的眼睑打量耕地和牧场。

天际的灰浆淡了，房屋

和山墙的白石灰浅了，

雄鸡很快就会吹响

起床号。

然后角落的裂隙处

有什么突然闯入。

唐纳利的左手抬起

又落在我的枪管上。这只属于他，

"看在上帝分上，"我气愤地说，"慢慢来，还有更多。"

一只花花公子兔蹦蹦跳跳来到

白蜡树旁的陷阱边。"今后不再是浪荡者，"[①]

唐纳利说着，清空双管弹药

并得手。

又一只沙锥鸟迅疾飞入空中，

一匹母马嘶鸣并颤动着腰臀

跑上山坡。三声枪响之后

---

① 来自一首流行的爱尔兰民歌。

其他动物不会回来。我们漫步

走向铁轨；当时的价钱很低

所以我们没有费事割去猎物的舌头。

警报解除后悄悄回来的兔子们

将最先把它查看。

在挖土豆现场

一

机械挖掘机摧毁田垄，
根与土的黑雨四处飞扬。
劳动者从后面蜂拥，弯躬
装满柳筐。手指在寒冷中冻僵。

像鸦群袭击鸦黑的田野，
散乱的队伍从树篱蔓延到田边；
总有一些人打乱破碎的队列，
为满载而归，然后起身挺直，站

一会儿但很快又踉跄着返回，
为从泥土的碎浪打捞新的一筐。
头低着，身弯下，双手摸索黑
母亲。俯身列队穿过草场

机械反复如秋天，百千年
以来对饥馑之神的怕与敬
磨砺他们卑膝之后的肌腱，

形成节令的土地祭坛。

二

燧石白，紫。它们散落
如鼓胀的卵石。泥土
黑笼的土生子，
对半的种子在那里萌芽成形，
这些眯眼的球形块茎仿佛
田垄石化的心。被铁锹
劈开，露出奶油白。

破碎的土壤散发好闻的气味。
粗砺的腐土表层喷涌出
簇簇土豆（洁净的诞生）
坚实的手感，潮湿的内部，
承诺根与土的味道。
将被堆在穴中：活骷髅，盲眼睛。

三

活骷髅，盲眼睛，摇晃
在扭曲的骨架上，

搜刮着四五年的土地①，
吞下染病的块根并死去。

新土豆，健全如石头，
也会腐烂，只消在
狭长的土穴里待上三天。
百千万土豆全都腐烂。

嘴闭紧，眼无神，
脸枯皱如拔毛的禽。
在百万间柳棚屋，
饥馑之喙啄食脏腑。

一个生来就挨饿的民族，
在泥土中，摸索，如植物，
嫁接于一种巨大的悲伤。
葫芦一样烂掉的希望。

恶臭的土豆污染土地，
穴将脓变为肮脏的圆冢：
在挖土豆者所在的地方，

———————————

① 指一八四五年。爱尔兰大饥荒，亦称土豆饥荒，大致在
一八四五至一八四九年间。

你依然能嗅到流脓的疮。

四

欢乐的鸥鸟舰队下
节奏渐逝，劳工暂停。
黑面包与鲜艳的罐装茶
是午餐。他们快累死了，扑通

坐在沟渠里饱餐充饥，
感恩地打破漫长的斋戒；
然后，伸展在不忠的土地，
倾冷茶为祭酒，撒面包屑。

给"伊丽莎"号轮船的中校

……其他人，面容枯槁，眼球凸出、瞪视，显然已极度饥饿。军官向詹姆斯·唐布雷恩爵士汇报情况……詹姆斯爵士"不合时宜地进行了干预"。劳斯写道。

塞茜尔·伍德姆-史密斯,《大饥荒》

在西梅奥附近海域例行巡航；见
一小船形迹可疑地远远
离港，我抢风航行并用盖尔语
制止船员。他们划桨的速度明显减弱，
逐渐停下，我猜，是出于
负疚或害怕，这时，我的天啊，
我们看见，他们的船底堆着
六个成年人，嘴巴张开，眼球
凸出眼眶如田垄里的洋葱。
六具面色苍白骨瘦如柴的活死人。
"啊，啊，
啊。"他们绝望的哀鸣与嚎叫
起起落落如一群饥饿的鸥鸟。
我们知道食物紧缺，但在船上

他们总能保障我们的面粉和牛肉，

所以，理解我的感受，以及水手们的，

没有指令让我们去救苦救难，

既然西部港口会提供救援——

尽管这些可怜的家伙显然活不到那时候。

我不得不拒绝给予食物：他们咒骂、咆哮

像被狠狠踢中私处的狗。

他们划着右侧的船桨向我逼近

（冒着翻船的风险）我看见他们

暴力而绝望。我张帆

躲开。多一事不如少一事。

第二天，像六种恶臭，那些活骷髅

穿过幽暗的架子床和舱门飘来，

一入港我就为我的船驱邪，

并向总检察官汇报这一切。

据我所知，詹姆斯爵士敦促无偿救济

西部港口片区的饥民，

却收获好白厅的尖刻斥责。

让当地人自食其力取得成功；

谁不会游泳谁就该淹死。

"海警过于热情积极了。"

我想，他们会这样说。

卜水者

从绿树篱割一根榛树杈
他握紧这 V 形的两端：
绕地三匝，猎捕水的
撩动，敏感，但熟练

而不乱。撩拨来得刺若针蜇。
树枝猝动，伴着精准的痉挛，
泉水突然通过绿榛枝
广播它的秘密基站。

旁观者也想一试。
他默默把树枝递到他们手中。
它在他们的紧握中死去，直至
他从容抓住人们企盼的手腕。榛枝颤动。

观火鸡

有人观察它们，有人垂涎它们；
冷漠的太平间里它们胸脯瘀青，
赤身搁浅于冰冷的大理石板
只穿着露骨的羽毛内衣花边。

鲜红的牛排尚且葆有
几分浓烈的生之庄严：
挂钩上的半幅乳牛也宣告
血肉之躯未受漠视。

但火鸡在死亡中畏缩。
揪它的脖，拔它的毛，瞧——
它不过是另一个可怜的分叉①家伙，
一个填满黑石灰的皮囊。

它也曾抱怨不休
发出咯咯的前奏；
它曾在布满爪印的污泥上发威

---

① 指禽类颈部与胸部之间的叉骨。

闪烁它孔夫子的灰眼睛。

如今，我经过凄清的圣诞灯光，
见它与它冰冷的飞友陈列一处：
机身赤裸，傲翼摧折，
剥光的尾翼仅余羞耻的舵。

怀孕的奶牛

她好像吞下了一只木桶。
从前腿到后臀，
她的肚子垂悬如吊床。

拍打她走出牛棚如同拍打
一大袋种子。我的手
仿佛被鞭打般疼痛，但我必须
持续不断地打她
并聆听击打声重重坠落如深水炸弹
在她深腹爆炸。

乳房膨胀。风笛的
气囊被塞进那里
为给她的哞哞声伴奏。
她的反刍她的乳，她的高潮她的犊
循环往复。

鳟　鱼

悬浮，肥美的枪管，
在拱桥下的深处
或如黄油滑下
河流的咽喉。

从平滑如李的深处，
它的枪口指向靶心；
瞄准草籽和飞蛾
个个歼灭，消失。

当河水冲泻
充满沙砾的河床
它被射出浅滩，
白鱼肚水平地

爆炸；如追踪弹
飞回石子之间
并且从未燃尽。
一阵冷血迸发

推波助澜。

瀑 布

小溪稳步淹没在自己的倾泻中，
一阵薄纱与玻璃的纷乱
戛然而止，飞流溅沫。

加速与骤减
同时进行；水流下
如恶人在尖叫中坠落接受审判。

像一个活跃的冰川
纵身折返：被吞没
又沿着狭长的咽喉回流。

我的目光追随它上穷碧落，追随
飞流直下的万钧瀑布落下，
落下，但记下这凝止的喧哗。

码头工人

那儿，角落里，盯视他的酒。
软帽突出像起重架的横梁，
罩住褶皱的前额和榔头般的下颌。
双唇如虎钳夹紧语言。

那拳头会给天主教徒挥上一锤——
哦，是的，这种事会再次发生。
他唯一能容忍的罗马领
是一品脱黑啤酒的柔滑泡沫。

马赛克的信念坚定如铆钉；
上帝是有些主见的工头，
让人生在劳逸之间变换。
工厂的喇叭将厉声宣告复活。

他坐着，强壮敦实如凯尔特十字，
显然习惯了沉默和扶手椅：
今晚，妻子和孩子们将保持安静，
当厅里传来摔门声和烟鬼的咳嗽。

城市教堂的穷女人

小小蜡炬融化发光，
在大理石上闪烁，把明亮
星火映在黄铜烛台：
右边的圣母祭坛上，
蓝火苗在烛芯上摇摆。

老妇人们头披黑纱、脸如面团
蜷缩跪在座席间。
蜡烛冰冷的黄火舌、蓝火苗
扭捏摇曳，当喃喃祈唤
飞向神圣的名号。

她们就这样每天在此
圣地跪拜。金色神龛，圣坛蕾丝，
大理石柱和清凉树荫
让她们平静。幽暗中你看不清来自
她们蜡黄额间的一丝皱纹。

引　力

高飞的风筝看似自由飘荡，

却受控于缰绳，拉紧且遁形。

那鸽子突然离开你去翱翔

此刻正在归家，本能地忠诚。

恋人们激烈争吵唇枪舌剑

往往伤害对方也伤害自己，

忍受绝望的一天，宣告他们的悔憾，

重返彼此臂弯的故港里。

乔伊斯在巴黎，失明且迷醉，

在聚会上点数奥康奈尔街①的一家家商店

爱奥纳岛的科伦西利②为寻求安慰

把爱尔兰的泥土佩在脚边。

---

① 爱尔兰首都都柏林最重要、最繁华的街道。

② 科伦西利（Colmcille，521–597），亦作圣高隆巴或科伦巴
（St Columba），其名字意为"教会之鸽"。著名的爱尔兰盖尔族
天主教僧侣与修道院院长，将基督教传播到皮克特人之中，是
将天主教传入苏格兰及爱尔兰的先驱。他在今日的苏格兰爱奥
那岛建立了修道院并长居于此，使其成为当时的宗教中心，因
此也被称为来自爱奥纳的高隆巴（Saint Columba of Iona）。他
被认为是爱尔兰十二使徒之一。

惊弓之鸟

她的围巾是芭铎风，
绒面平底鞋便于散步，
某晚她来到我身边
为吹吹风也为友好倾诉。
我们穿过静静的河，
走上堤岸小路。

车流屏住呼吸，
天空如绷紧的心膜：
暮色像一块幕布
因天鹅游动而瑟缩，
战栗如盘旋的鹰
致命，静默。

必要的真空
摧毁每一颗猎心
但我们战栗着保持
鹰与猎物的距离，
保留古典的得体，
谈笑间充满技艺。

青春的教训
教我俩学会静候，
不表露感情
以免追悔莫及——
闪电恋爱已经
演变为反目成仇。

所以，谨慎且兴奋
如歌鸫被猎鹰挽住，
我们为三月的暮光激动
伴着紧张稚嫩的倾诉：
静水方能流深
沿着堤岸小路。

告 别

穿着花边衬衫、
简单格裙的夫人
自从你离开这家园，
它的虚空侵损
心神。你在这里，
时光平顺，笑靥
为锚；而你的缺席
摇晃爱的天平，松解
时日的缆绳。光阴
在日历上颠簸，
只因再也不闻
你柔如花朵
的安恬嗓音。热望击打我的海岸；
你走后，我如堕烟海。
在你重发号令前，
自我陷入哗变。

阿伦岛的恋人们

永恒的海浪，明亮、淘沥的碎玻璃，
光辉耀目地涌来，涌入礁岩，
烟波粼粼地涌来，经美洲淘洗

只为占据阿伦岛。抑或阿伦岛奔去
抛出宽广的岩臂拥抱潮水，
后者屈服地退潮、轻柔地撞击？

大海界定陆地还是陆地界定大海？
彼此都从浪的碰撞中汲取新意。
大海撞击陆地以圆成自身。

诗

给玛丽

亲爱的，我将为你完善这孩子
他在我的脑海里勤勉而闲散
用沉重的铁锹挖掘直到草泥堆积
或在深沟里打滚满身泥团。

每年我都在一码长的菜园种地。
我会锄一层草皮筑一堵墙
为了阻挡母猪和啄食的母鸡。
每年，尽管如此，草墙塌方。

或高兴地在黏黏的淤泥内
泼溅并在流动的水渠上筑堤，
但我那黏土和烂泥的堡垒
总熬不过秋天的雨季。

亲爱的，你要为我完善这孩子
他将不断突破不完善的小局限：
在新的界限内，规划世界，
在我们的四壁中，在我们的金指环。

蜜月飞行

下方，大地的拼图，围篱的黑边，
公路长长的灰丝带将村落与田野
系缚或松开于闲适的联姻：
我们在小湖和农庄上方倾斜，

当我们攀升，离开熟悉的景色，
确定的绿世界开始倾覆。
发动机的噪音改变。你望我。
海岸线从机翼末端淡出。

被火的力量发射离地，
我们悬浮着，奇迹般，在水上，
依赖那无影无形的空气
使我们飘浮，载我们去远方。

我们前方的天空正遭遇气浪。
一个平静的声音说起云而我们茫然。
气囊摇晃恐惧，我们下降。
旅人啊，此时此刻，唯有信任。

脚手架

泥瓦匠，当他们开始盖房子，
他们会小心翼翼地测试架子；

确保木板不会在忙碌中滑落，
放稳所有悬梯，加固螺栓接合。

然而这一切都将在完工时拆掉，
以展现一面面石墙的坚实稳牢。

所以，我亲爱的，假如有时啊，
你我之间的旧桥梁看似崩塌，

别怕。就让那脚手架倾倒，
相信我们的墙已经筑好。

岛上风暴

我们有备而来：我们建低矮的房子，

把墙建在基岩，屋顶用上好的石板。

这沧桑大地从不用干草骚扰

我们，所以，你看，不会有草垛

或麦秆丢失的风险。也没有树木

可以为伴，当岛上突然暴风

骤雨：你懂我的意思——树叶树枝

能在飓风中扬起悲哀的和鸣

让你聆听你所恐惧的东西

忘记它也在击打你的房屋。

但是没有树，没有天然的荫蔽。

你也许觉得大海是伴侣，

在悬崖峭壁上快意地炸裂，

然而不：风袭时，飞溅的浪花击打

一扇扇窗户，嘶鸣如一只家猫

变得野蛮。当狂风俯冲并隐身扫射，

我们原地不动。空间里万箭齐发，

我们被虚空的空气狂轰滥炸。

多奇怪，我们怕的是浩大的虚无。

阿伦岛的辛格[①]

海挥发的盐磨砺
四方来风的刃，
剥去大片
喀斯特岩，腐蚀
干枯的大地表层；
悬崖被磨出
圆角。

    岛民也
被雕刻。留意
那尖刻的怒容，嘴巴
雕成上翻的锚，
光滑的脑袋
充满溺水。

      看啊，
他来了，刚硬的笔

[①] 约翰·辛格（John Millington Synge，1871–1909），爱尔兰戏剧家、诗人、民间文学收集者，爱尔兰文学复兴运动的重要人物。代表作有《西方世界的花花公子》，在都柏林首演时引起骚乱。与叶芝、格雷戈里夫人共同创建了艾比剧院（Abbey Theatre）。辛格患病期间，叶芝建议他前往阿伦岛疗养。

在他脑中刮擦；

笔尖在咸风中磨砺，

浸入呜咽的海水。

圣弗朗西斯与鸟群

当弗朗西斯布道"爱"给鸟群,
它们倾听,盘旋,加速
飞上蓝天如一群诗文

从他圣洁的唇间放出只为好玩。
然后迅速转回,在他头顶嗡鸣,
在修士斗篷上单脚旋转,

空中起舞,为单纯的欢乐
嬉戏唱歌,如一群意象飞腾。
这是弗朗西斯的最佳诗作,

他的论点真实,他的语调轻盈。

在小镇

给柯林·米德尔顿 [①]

在小镇他的猪鬃画笔

从黏土中分离花岗岩

直到岩石中水晶裸露：

饱含颜料的画笔磨砺

青山与灰石楠的边缘。

地表岩石收缩，不敢对视。

光谱引爆，像明亮的榴弹，

当他开始解锁保险扣

画晨露，画云朵，画雨。

裂成碎片的光束像铁铲

除去土地的朦胧和斑驳，

洁净如骨，残忍如痛

一场剧烈的心脏病。

他的眼，贪婪的厚镜片，钻燧

光秃的大地，染上白与红，

---

① 柯林·米德尔顿（Colin Middleton，1910-1983），北爱尔兰
超现实主义画家。

焚烧它直至它幽冥

而绚烂如葬礼上的柴堆：

一个新世界从他脑中冷凝。

民歌手

循环播放被时光循环的歌词，
把每一首沧桑的歌
嵌入新刻的密纹和声，
他们娴熟地拨弦并摇摆
一颗悲伤之心的平衡。

麻木的激情，在乡村爱情的羞涩
螺壳里缓缓凝成珍珠，
串于一支脆弱的曲调，
如今那么刺眼，搔首弄姿
像每一个刚进城的乡巴佬。

他们预制的故事出售
上万次：苍白的爱情
浓妆艳抹招摇过市。哼唱
焊接所有心碎。死神的利刃
在令人麻醉的弹拨中颓钝。

游戏的方式

阳光穿透玻璃，摸索每一张书案
搜寻奶瓶、吸管和陈旧的干面包皮。
音乐阔步发出挑战，
将回忆和欲念混在粉笔灰里。

我的教案上写着：教师播放
贝多芬的《第五协奏曲》，
学生通过写作自由地表达
自己。一个说："我们可以摇摆吗？"

当我播放唱片时；但此刻，
巨大的声响使他们安静。更高昂，
更坚定，每一个威严的音符
给教室鼓气如饱满的轮胎，

在睁大的眼睛后实施它私密的
咒语。他们一度忘了我的
存在。奋笔疾书，念念有词，
笨拙地拥抱自由的

词语。一种甜蜜的静默

在迷茫的脸上乍现，我看见

新的面貌。然后音符收紧如圈套。他们

不知不觉坠入自己。

私有的赫利孔

给迈克尔·朗利[①]

小时候，他们不能让我远离水井

和带有水桶与辘轳的老水泵。

我爱那幽暗的沉落，被困的天空，

还有水草、真菌和湿苔藓的气息。

有一口井，在砖厂，盖板腐化。

我喜欢品味那丰沛的击荡声

当水桶从绳梢骤然落下。

那么深，你看不见里面的倒影。

干砌石渠下有一口浅井

和任何鱼塘一样茂密。

当你从柔软的腐土拽出长长的根须，

一张白脸盘旋在水底。

另一些有回声，传回你自己的呼唤

---

①迈克尔·朗利（Michael Longley，1939– ），与希尼同代的诗
人、朋友。二十世纪六十年代与希尼一同参加贝尔法斯特诗人
小组，定期分享、讨论诗歌。

伴着崭新的音乐。有一口井
很可怕，因为，透过蕨类和高高的
毛地黄，一只老鼠掠过我的倒影。

如今，去窥探根须，用手指触摸淤泥，
去注视，如大眼睛的纳西索斯，注视泉井
有损成人的尊严。我写诗
为了看清自己，让黑暗发出回声。

进入黑暗之门

1969

给我的父亲母亲

目 录

致　谢

一些诗曾发表在以下报刊上，谨向这些报刊的编辑致谢：

《都柏林杂志》、《诚实的阿尔斯特人》、《爱尔兰日报》、《爱尔兰时报》、《倾听者》、《新政治家》、《前哨》、《凤凰》、《泰晤士报文学增刊》、《大学评论》以及 BBC 北爱尔兰。《献给短发党人的安魂曲》中的一些细节来自 P. 奥凯利的《一七九八年叛乱通史》(都柏林，1842)。

夜 景

一定要重温吗？
干草上沉重的脚步声，
不安的嘶鸣。

海绵唇露出每一颗孤立的牙齿。
斑驳的腰臀，
肌肉和马蹄

困在屋顶下。

逝

绿唾液在闪亮的衔铁

两端起泡

那是牧草灰的遗迹。

汗湿、扭曲的腹带

如今僵硬，摸着冰冷，

两片眼罩垫

中央隆起。

辔头、锁链和缰绳

缠绕垂下。

他的热臭消失了。

这地方只留下他熟悉的霉味。

他走得匆忙

只穿着马掌

连马厩都没收拾。

梦

我拿着钩镰

它手铸的端头很重

我用它砍一棵茎

茎粗如电线杆。

我的袖子卷起

凉风拂过手臂

我先挥刀入土，

再将它用力拔出。

下一刀，

在钩下发现一颗人头。

醒来前

我听见钢刀停在

额骨的声音。

不法之徒

凯利养了一头非法公牛，远离
公路：如果奶牛在那里配种

你冒着被罚的风险也要付正常的报酬。
我曾用绳索拖一头紧张的荷兰奶牛

走下一条赤杨和杨絮的小巷，
走向那个关着公牛的棚房。

我递给老凯利湿漉漉的银币，尽管猜
不出为何。他冷冷地嘟哝着："过来。

爬到栅栏上。"从高处的位置
我观看这场交易般的繁殖。

门，没上闩，砰然向后撞在墙隅。
不法之牛从他的棚里摸索出去

不慌不忙如老式蒸汽火车在轨道间更替。
他转圈，咕哝，嗅探。没有急促的喘吸，

轻松自如仿佛一位老练的商贩；
然后，突然一个笨拙的跳蹿，

他圆滚滚的前腿跨上她的腰腹
一步到位射入生命，坦克般冷酷，

落地如一拖斗沙砾倾荡。
"行了，"凯利说着，用桉杖

轻拍她的后部。"要是不行，带她回来。"
我走在她前面，此时绳子松开，

而凯利戳戳他的不法之徒，欢呼尖叫，
而公牛，享受自己的闲暇，回归黑暗、稻草。

钓鲑鱼者致鲑鱼

你噘着嘴逆流而上，再度
向内陆狂游，在故乡水流的
引力作用下，你的海上放逐
　　被无条件取消。

　　我站在水中央，抛钩。
脚下涨满的河水倒映
抛出的鱼钩、渔网和一只白手
　　轻撒色彩斑斓的饵蝇。

　　沃顿认为花园的蠕虫，若染着
暗黑常青藤浆果的油脂芳香
是对你最佳的诱惑，但此刻
　　你眼中的饥渴让你遭了殃。

　　涟漪在我周围迅速漾动，
急流把河水溅到我腿上，
置身于大河的舞步中
　　我行动，和你一样，凭借拉力和波光

并在你拉钩时拉钩，杀绝。

我们因为饵蝇同归于尽。

你无法抵御喉间的钢铁。

我也将回家，满身鱼腥、鱼鳞。

铁匠铺

我所知的全部是一扇进入黑暗之门。

屋外，旧轴承和铁环在生锈；

屋内，被锤击的铁砧短促鸣奏，

不可预料的扇形火花

或新马掌入水凝固的咝响。

铁砧想必位于房屋正中，

一端尖如独角兽，一端方正，

在那里岿然不动：一座祭堂

任由他为形状和音乐献身。

有时，他穿着皮围裙，鼻毛丛生，

倚着门框，在风驰电掣的

车流中忆起哒哒马蹄；

然后嘟哝着进屋，重一下轻一下

为打出真铁，让风箱轰鸣。

搭茅草屋顶的人

预约了几星期，某天早上他突然
出现，他的自行车上挂着
一个轻便梯子和一袋刀具。
他看看旧屋顶，戳戳屋檐，

打开并搬弄一捆捆扎紧的麦秸。
接着，是一捆捆枝条：掂量
榛枝柳枝的分量，扭一扭，看会不会折断。
整个早上他好像只是在热身：

然后搭好梯子，拿出磨利的刀
剪断麦秆，削尖枝条
然后，对折成白色的 U 形钉
一捧捧，把他的世界固定。

连续数日蹲在房椽上方的草皮，
他把麦秆粗端打磨，剪齐，缝成
一个倾斜的蜂巢，一片收割后的麦地，
让众人惊叹他的米达斯神技。

半 岛

当你再无更多可说，那便驱车
环岛兜风一整天。
天宇高远如跑道上空，
大地无迹所以你永不抵达

而是穿行，尽管始终接近陆地。
黄昏时，地平线饮尽山海，
犁过的田野吞噬白灰山墙，
你再度陷入黑暗。那么回忆

上釉的前滩和浮木的剪影，
有波涛碎在上面的暗礁，
长腿海鸟仿佛踩着高跷，
岛屿安然遁入迷雾。

然后开车回家，依然无话可说
但你现在能破解一切风景，
以此原则：事物纯粹建立于自身的形状，
海水和陆地处在各自的极境。

在加拉鲁斯礼拜堂

你依然能感到僧众挤满
此地：像走进堆叠的泥炭，
古老的黑暗之心被一码厚的岩石
围起。当你独自置身其中，
你，一个退化的生物，可能坠入
地球深处。没有哪个朝拜者
能跃出这地面奔向他的上帝。

如古墓中的英雄矗立在那里，
他们在他们的王的眼中寻找自我
承受自己呼吸的黑色压迫。
当他们走出，他曾怎样对他们微笑，
大海为香炉，青草作火焰。

戏水的女孩们，高威，一九六五年

她们在海沫中漂浮嬉游，
手臂组成凯瑟琳之轮焰火；
每个脑袋快速弹跳像足球。
尖叫声在海滨上听来微弱。

从来没有玉臂的维纳斯
神奇地诞生在这西部海滨。
在我们更冷峻的神话中
海盗女王身披战衣。海浪

将自己倾入自己，年华
在空间穿梭了无痕迹。
浪尖展开如啤酒沫
女王的衣装泯没海里

而一代代人在海浪
击碎的咸沤中叹息
怀着对肉与罪的恐惧劳作
因为日期满了。

穿着泳衣涉过浅滩，

赤裸的腿，光滑的肩，颀长的背，

她们又跳又叫涉水上岸。

维纳斯来了，真实不虚。

献给短发党人的安魂曲

我们的大衣口袋塞满麦粒——

奔逃中没有厨房，没有拔营——

我们在自己的国度快速突然地转移。

阴沟后牧师与流浪汉躺在一起。

一个民族，说不上行军——而是长途行走——

我们每天都有新的战术发生：

我们用长枪斩断缰绳和骑手

并让牛群惊慌四散冲击步兵，

然后从树篱撤退因为在那里骑兵必然绊倒。

直到，醋山上，那场致命的秘密会晤。

数千人成排死去，用镰刀挥向大炮。

我们的冲击波浸红山麓。

他们埋了我们，没有裹尸布或棺材

八月，新生的大麦钻出坟墓。

春之祭

于是严冬握拳
把拳头卡在水泵。
活塞在它的喉中

冻成一个肿块，冰铸在
铁上。水泵的手柄
倾斜地瘫痪。

然后把麦秸
拧成绳，紧紧缠绕
泵身和喷头，然后一根火柴

让水泵着了火。
它冷下来，我们拉起她的闩扣，
她的入口潮湿，她来了。

水　妖

他披荆斩棘，铲除灰泥
赋予我在自己沟渠的通行权
而我飞奔向他，洗去锈迹。

他停下，见我终于完全袒露，
清澈流淌，显然漫不经心。
于是他从我身旁走过。我荡漾我翻腾

河边沟渠纵横
直到他一铲掘入我深腹
将我占据。我吞下他的沟渠

心满意足，为了爱，将自己驱散到
他的根底，爬上他的黄铜纹理——
而一旦他知道我喜欢，唯有我

能给他微妙的涨潮和反射。
他从头到尾打探我，让我四肢
失去冰冷的自由。有了人性，对他产生热情。

妻子的故事

我在树篱下铺上亚麻布
摆好食物，招呼他们过来。
打谷机的轰鸣与吞咽声减弱
大传输带戛然而止，还没
来得及传送的麦秆悬在口中。
如此安静以至于我能听见二十码外
他们的靴子踏在残梗间的咯吱声。

他躺下来说："先给大伙儿，
我不急。"拔下一把把青草
抛向空中。"看起来不错。"
（他朝我铺在草地上的白桌布点头。）
"我敢说女人能把整片田野都摆满
尽管我们男人并不需要桌布。"
他眨眨眼，然后看着我把杯子斟满
并在他喜欢的厚面包片上涂黄油。
"打谷的效果比我想的好，瞧，
那可是干净的良种。去那儿看看。"
这样的视察永远不会少，
尽管看什么我从不知道。

但我还是把手伸进凹槽边

那些半满的麻袋。谷粒坚硬如子弹，

无数且冰冷。麻袋张着口，

滑运道朝后伸向静止的滚筒，

耙子倾斜插在地上

像标枪标记失落的战场。

我穿过它们返回，经过麦梗。

他们躺在各自的食物碎屑间

抽烟，不说话。"丰收啦，

不是吗？"——骄傲得仿佛他就是土地本身——

"磨面播种全都管够。"

就这样。我来了，他给我看了，

这儿就没我的事了。

我收拾杯子，叠好桌布，

离开。但他们还悠哉悠哉，

舒展，敞怀，满足地，在树下。

母　亲

我在水泵边劳作，强风
夹着细雨磨损
我汲水的井绳。
随着活塞的每一次豪饮，
绳索松开像空气的胎盘。

我厌倦了给牲畜喂食。
每晚我在这手柄旁劳作，
每次半个钟，奶牛
在牛棚的碗边狂饮。
我还没来得及把碗装满，
它们已把水喝低。

它们又无精打采地进去了，从那扇他钉在
篱笆上的简易门：那是叮当响的床头架
被铁丝绑在门柱间。摇摇欲坠，
不再发出欢乐的叮当。

我厌倦了拖着体内这个活塞
走动。上帝啊，他就像一只小牛犊

扯着绳子疯狂地蹦跳。
躺着站着都不能平息这些跃动，
我井中的豪饮。

哦，当我是自己的一扇门
就让这风磨损我的羊水
正如它嵌接我腿间的裙摆，
把空气塞入我的咽喉。

重访迦南

这里没有圆润的陶罐，没有服务员
照顾人们的消耗或供给
锁在阀门后的水示意
不要期待神奇的语言。

但在这酵母般膨胀的骨骼支撑的子宫，
完好的纯贞有待示迹，
美妙的祝圣礼（属于他们自己）
一如宴会上的水变成酒红。

挽歌：给一个流产的孩子

一

你妈妈步履轻盈像一个空竹笼
努力忘却你曾经亲密的触碰

那是你胚芽血肉和胶状骨骼绑在一起的重量
强加于她。那个被清空的世界

收缩，围绕它的历史，它的伤痛。
末日到来，你崩塌的行星

陨灭在我们的大气层，
你妈妈为她体内的轻而感到沉重。

二

你做了六个月的绘图人，
指引我的朋友从丈夫走向父亲。

他猜中有一颗星球在你稳固的圆丘中。
然后地极陨落，流星，落空。

三

孤独的旅途中我思索这一切，
死之生，为了埋葬的开掘，

小衣服做的花环，婴儿车作为纪念，
父母伸出手去触及一条肢体的幻感。

我自动驾驶在这空荡的路上
在微雨的天空下，秃鸦盘旋，

越过山野，云雾弥漫，
冬日的湖上白浪归家。

维多利亚时代的吉他

给戴维·哈蒙德 [①]

铭文:"曾属于路易莎·凯瑟琳·库伊,在她嫁给
约翰·查尔斯·史密斯之前,一八五二年三月。"

我原以为铭文记载
馈赠日期,类似某种洗礼:
这却像棺材上的铭牌。

路易莎·凯瑟琳·库伊不会轻松。
在初夜被取消的
远非少女的名姓。

我相信他感受不到你的抚摸
就像这把琴——因为很明显
约翰·查尔斯手指并不灵敏——

显然是女士的琴:
共鸣箱苗条如紧身衣女孩,

---

① 戴维·哈蒙德(David Hammond,1928–2008),北爱尔兰作
家、音乐家、历史学家、教师。希尼一家的好友。

琴颈适合最小的指距。

身为人妻，你可曾追踪它的下落？
你可知道它现在的主人
正带给它一生中最大的快乐？

夜晚驱车

寻常事物的气息
在夜晚驱车穿越法国时更新：
空气中的雨水、干草和树林
在敞篷车里形成暖流。

路标不断变白。
蒙特利尔，阿布维尔，博韦
被应许，应许，来了又去，
每个地方都兑现其名字的承诺。

一台联合收割机很晚还在一路呻吟
流泻的种子划过工作灯。
一场林火暗暗地烧尽。
一家家小咖啡馆相继关门。

我时时刻刻想着你
在千里外的南方，意大利
在黑暗的星球上把腰贴近法兰西。
你的寻常在那里更新。

在阿德博角

沿着那片湖滨
蚊蚋如烟云
浓密地飘在夕阳中。

它们轻盈地粉碎
在挡风玻璃上，
排气口和引擎盖在无数次

碰撞下沙沙作响：
仿佛开车穿过
一阵微细的谷壳雨。

但我们没留下清晰的航迹
因为它们随着空气的开合
在我们周围张翕。

今晚当我们熄灭灯光
在床上亲吻
它们依稀可闻的警笛

将在窗外响起，
它们隐形的纱幔
让月光更加暗淡，

墙壁会留下它们的
红疹，绿花粉。
到早上它们将渗透我们的衣裳。

如果你把一只放在显微镜下
你会看到一个鼓胀之身
翅膀是巨大的拍击器

以至于这场天罚或许
比法老的遭遇还要猛烈。
人们告诉我它们是蚊子

但要有森林和沼泽
我才相信
因为这是我们无辜的巡回

唱诗班，死在
它们自己鲜活的苍穹，唯一的烦恼是，
它们是舞者最后的面纱。

记忆的遗物

这些湖水
能点木成石：
旧桨和梁柱
经年累月
坚硬了纹理，
囚禁汁液

与风味的幽灵。
浅水拍岸
互相迁就：
持续的洗礼，
这淹没一切的爱
把树桩

惊为石笋。
死熔岩，
冷却的星，
煤炭与钻石
或烧焦的流星
突然降生

都太过简单，
缺少遗物
蕴藏的诱惑——
一枚石子
在学校的架上，
燕麦色。

内伊湖组诗

给渔夫

1. 在沿岸

一

湖水每年要一个祭品。

它能把木硬化为石。

水底有一座沉落的小镇。

那是马恩岛留下的疤痕。

二

在图姆桥，湖水奔向海洋

他们用新闸和鱼池挡住水流。

他们一次次打断鳗鱼的回航，

一口气举起五百石渔获。

三

但在安特里姆和蒂龙沿岸

这竞技中有几分公平。

渔夫们和鳗鱼单挑作战，

驶出数里且从不识水性。

四

"我们将更快沉没，"他们说。

而当你辩称这里风平浪静，

说漂浮一小时后他们肯定安全上岸——

"湖水每年要一个祭品。"

2. 超越马尾藻海

一个腺体搅动

内陆两百里的

淤泥，一汪水

叠着水向河口

逆流而行，在穿越

大西洋的途中，

从漂浮到游动，

确定如卫星

对海洋的

秘密引力，也忠于

自己的轨迹。

迎着

落潮，水流，礁石，险滩，

肌肉强健的冰凌

把自己融化得更长

更肥，淹埋

它的抵达

于光与潮水之外，

使淤泥和沙土

有了光滑的根。白天，

只有掘渠者的

铁锹和淤泥搅拌桨
能使它流产。黑夜
接引它，饥渴地
追随每一次波动。

3. 诱 饵

灯盏在午夜的田野里游荡。

三个男人凭直觉走在草间，

灯的光束是他们的船头和罗盘。

桶柄这时最好不要咔嗒响：

静寂与奇怪的光吸引饵虫。

捉住它，但要等

那最初的退缩，大拇指黏糊糊。

让它重新退回它的穴。

然后持续拉，它就会钻出。

数百万条在露湿的树叶和低垂的草尖下

盘结它们泥土的冠冕，

其中有些注定要在夜袭中被劫，

大地无辜的通风机，

与地球成为完美搭档，

其中一些注定上当

当灯盏在午夜的田野里游荡，

当渔夫们要为月桂献上花束

捉住它，在它必来的地方，来自尘土。

4. 放 线

一

渔线消失在视野外、心神外
坠入水底柔软的沙石与泥泞
越过猎捕之手漫不经心的技能。

盘绕在船尾的一束小钩
被缓缓放开，恢复原形，
直到钩束隐藏在虫中。

小船向前而渔线后倾。
双桨在托架里不停兜圈。
鳗鱼无声勾勒它的弧线。

二

鸥鸟飞翔并伞开在头上，
线一放尽就盘踞空中，
小船上方机敏的侍僧。

渔夫不懂《垂怜经》，
他们不知也从不尝试，

只把手中活计当作宿命。

他们清理桶内最后的残虫，
高高抛起，如释重负，一阵泥土雨。
鸥鸟先于湖水将它们吞噬。

5. 收 线

他们在满载的船上忙碌，
船朝着安特里姆潜行，电力中断。
烟灰色游丝般的渔线

被手忙脚乱地拉上船
每三码就有鱼钩被躲闪
或咬中（烟灰色变粗，手腕

那么粗，像脱粒机
被一股脑甩入
桶中）。每条鳗鱼

上船时都受到这种欢迎：
钩留在鳃里或牙龈，
啪地丢进桶中，摔晕

但把自己拧成四股，
与蜷缩、光滑的
渔获织成鱼背和灰肚的结

始终保持一体，

因为每条新丢进来的猎物

都像润滑油般被吸入。

而航迹在清晨的水域

彼此交织如渔获：哪个

船是哪个？

而这一切始于何时？

今早，去年，湖水初次产卵？

船员们会答："一旦时节来临。"

6. 回 归

在池塘、水渠和死运河，

她调转她的头，

长大了，从容地

跟着感觉走

直到置身藻海

并义无反顾，否则

又是新的沟渠，下水道，

沼泽，激流，湖泊，

河水。她的肚

收缩，她在水中

兴奋。水的脉动

是穿过时日的速度。

谁知道她现在是否知道

她的深度或方向？

她已经过马林角和

托里湾，无声，无迹，

一缕，一根灯芯，

它自己的烛与光，

穿过翻滚的黑暗。

一旦在海底一万尺

她的发源地产卵，

她就消亡。水流

承载片片孤卵。

7. 幻 象

除非他把头发梳好，

否则，他们说，虱子会结成

一股粉质的绳

把他，又小又脏，在劫难逃，

拖入水中。于是

他在河岸的田边

小心谨慎。缆绳粗如桦树干，

每当有风吹过

便在草中绷紧。多年

之后在同样的田野

他在夜晚伫立，当鳗鱼

穿过草丛如被孵化的隐患

游向水里。伫立

在一处，当田野流

过，一条咯喱路，

观望鳗鱼穿越陆地

重新缠绕他的世界的活腰带。

磷光闪闪、肌肉强健的淤泥

在他脚下持续行进。光阴

验证可怖的缆绳。

天赐之音

在布拉斯基特群岛最西端
一间石垒小屋里
他从黑夜获得此曲。

后来也有人听到
奇异的噪声，曲调的碎片
在呼啸的天气中来临

只是不成旋律。
他责备他们的手指和耳朵
缺乏训练，他们的演奏随意，

因为他曾只身入岛
并带回全部的一切。
房屋搏动像他拉满的提琴。

所以，他是否称之为灵乐
我并不在意。他从
大西洋中部的风里将它采撷。

他甚至认为，无迹可寻。

它自琴弓庄严涌出，

将自己重新组织成乐曲。

荆豆地

荆豆一整年
能开一两朵花
但此刻它盛放。
仿佛春天所有鸟巢

所有鸟蛋的
小小蛋黄斑点
被尖尖地高悬
在灌木各处等待成熟。

山丘氧化黄金。
在青枝焖烧的烟云
和脚下死棘的余烬
之上，荆豆花灼人。

在荆豆下放一根
火柴，它们迅速引燃。
阳光下没有火焰
而是热的剧震。

然而那样的焚烧

仅吞噬荆棘——

坚韧的枝条烧不尽，

幸存如骨，烧焦的兽角。

镀金，多刺，柔韧，褶皱，

这发育不良的、干枯的丰饶

顽强在山野，在石壕，

在燧石床和战场。

种植园

林中任何一点
都是中心，白桦干
幽灵般萦绕你的方位，
即兴画出魔法环

无论你停在哪里。
尽管你走的是直线，
你也可能兜了圈，
毒蘑菇和矮树桩

始终反复出现。
抑或你重遇它们？
这里有越橘覆盖土地，
一场大火的黑烬，

而一旦发现它们，
你就注定再次发现。
总有人曾在那里
尽管你总是孤单。

恋人们，观鸟者，

露营者，吉卜赛人，流浪汉

留下他们的行迹

或粪便。

树篱茂密遮蔽大路，

它却欢迎所有来者

随着低语的踏车

进入寂静与柔软，

他们以为，

它与外部界限分明。

他们一定很感激

车水马龙的轰鸣

如果他们冒险

越过野餐区

或开始想起

山雾的传说。

你必须回来

才能学会迷失自己，

领航员兼迷途者——巫师，

汉塞尔与格蕾特合一。[1]

---

[1] 汉塞尔与格蕾特是格林童话中的兄妹，被邪恶的继母抛弃林中。汉塞尔沿路丢下白卵石作为标记，以便他和格蕾特找到回家的路。

海岸线

转过拐角，登上小山
在唐恩郡，大海
潜行并安顿
在树篱后。或者

灰色前滩上的水潭
无神如鱼目。
随机的潮汐旋涡界定
麦田和牧场。

环绕安特里姆向西
在两百里外的莫赫
玄武岩备战迎敌。
海洋与海峡

都在爱尔兰的黑闸
溅起浮沫。而海滨
在呜咽中归顺
威克洛与梅奥。

无论何时。海潮
都肆虐
所有田野低处，
所有峭壁和卵石。

听。是不是丹麦人，
盘踞风帆的黑鹰？
或金戈铁马的诺曼人？
还是沼泽高高跃起

占领那边的沙滩？
斯特兰福德，阿克洛，卡里克弗格斯，
贝尔马利特和文特里
尚在，被遗忘如哨岗。

班恩河黏土

劳作者轻松地骑车
经过小巷尽头
全身染白。工装裤
和靴子也沾着粉末。

他们整日在露天开采场
把厚土块装运到河岸
像一块块四方
蓝色奶油。沉陷

在草丛下数百岁，
它在阳光中烘白，
释放出贮藏的水
开始成熟。

它潜流在河谷下，
是一条探路之河
最初缓释的沉渣。
在它上方，错综的沼泽是新的，

甚至那堆中石器时代的燧石
也是。一次，当我清理水渠，
我铲起黏性的浮质
直到水渐渐清晰

流淌在古老的河床。
腐殖质和根须下
这平滑的重量。我依然
朝着它努力。它持续而充盈。

沼泽地

给 T. P. 弗拉纳根^①

我们没有草原
在傍晚切割巨日——
到处，目光让步于
逼近的地平线，

被诱入山中小湖的
巨人独眼。我们不设防的国度
是沼泽不断结痂
在日升日落之间。

他们从泥炭中取出
爱尔兰大麋鹿
骨架，重新立起，
一个惊人的板条箱装满空气。

一百多年前
沉埋的黄油
重现咸味和洁白。

---

① T. P. 弗拉纳根（T. P. Flanagan, 1929–2011），爱尔兰风景画家。

大地本身仁慈，黑黄油

在脚下融化并敞开，
距它最后定型
还有数百万年。
他们永不在此挖煤，

只有巨杉树干
浸在水中，柔软如纸浆。
我们的开拓者不断击掘，
向内，向下。

他们剥掉的每一层
似都有栖居的遗迹。
沼泽穴或许是大西洋的渗漏。
潮湿的中央深不见底。

Death of a Naturalist

Charlie Witherspoon interviews young Heaney, who reads
"The Waterfall" from *Death of a Naturalist*, 1966

For Marie

Contents

Acknowledgements are due to the editors of the following, in which some of these poems have appeared:

Belfast Telegraph, *Dublin Magazine*, *Kilkenny Magazine*, *Interest*, *Irish Times*, *The Listener*, *New Statesman*, *Northern Review*, *Outposts*, *Poetry Ireland*, *Vogue*, *The Arts in Ulster* (BBC Northern Ireland), *The Living Poet* and *The Poet's Voice* (BBC Third Programme); Universities Poetry 5, Young Commonwealth Poets '65 (Heinemann).

Digging

Between my finger and my thumb
The squat pen rests; snug as a gun.

Under my window, a clean rasping sound
When the spade sinks into gravelly ground:
My father, digging. I look down

Till his straining rump among the flowerbeds
Bends low, comes up twenty years away
Stooping in rhythm through potato drills
Where he was digging.

The coarse boot nestled on the lug, the shaft
Against the inside knee was levered firmly.
He rooted out tall tops, buried the bright edge deep
To scatter new potatoes that we picked,
Loving their cool hardness in our hands.

By God, the old man could handle a spade.
Just like his old man.

My grandfather cut more turf in a day
Than any other man on Toner's bog.
Once I carried him milk in a bottle
Corked sloppily with paper. He straightened up
To drink it, then fell to right away

Nicking and slicing neatly, heaving sods
Over his shoulder, going down and down
For the good turf. Digging.

The cold smell of potato mould, the squelch and slap
Of soggy peat, the curt cuts of an edge
Through living roots awaken in my head.

But I've no spade to follow men like them.

Between my finger and my thumb
The squat pen rests.
I'll dig with it.

Death of a Naturalist

All year the flax-dam festered in the heart
Of the townland; green and heavy headed
Flax had rotted there, weighted down by huge sods.
Daily it sweltered in the punishing sun.
Bubbles gargled delicately, bluebottles
Wove a strong gauze of sound around the smell.
There were dragon-flies, spotted butterflies,
But best of all was the warm thick slobber
Of frogspawn that grew like clotted water
In the shade of the banks. Here, every spring,
I would fill jampotfuls of the jellied
Specks to range on window-sills at home,
On shelves at school, and wait and watch until
The fattening dots burst into nimble-
Swimming tadpoles. Miss Walls would tell us how
The daddy frog was called a bullfrog,
And how he croaked, and how the mammy frog
Laid hundreds of little eggs and this was
Frogspawn. You could tell the weather by frogs too
For they were yellow in the sun and brown
In rain.

   Then one hot day when fields were rank
With cowdung in the grass, the angry frogs
Invaded the flax-dam; I ducked through hedges
To a coarse croaking that I had not heard
Before. The air was thick with a bass chorus.
Right down the dam, gross-bellied frogs were cocked
On sods; their loose necks pulsed like sails. Some hopped:
The slap and plop were obscene threats. Some sat
Poised like mud grenades, their blunt heads farting.
I sickened, turned, and ran. The great slime kings
Were gathered there for vengeance, and I knew
That if I dipped my hand the spawn would clutch it.

The Barn

Threshed corn lay piled like grit of ivory
Or solid as cement in two-lugged sacks.
The musty dark hoarded an armoury
Of farmyard implements, harness, plough-socks.

The floor was mouse-grey, smooth, chilly concrete.
There were no windows, just two narrow shafts
Of gilded motes, crossing, from air-holes slit
High in each gable. The one door meant no draughts

All summer when the zinc burned like an oven.
A scythe's edge, a clean spade, a pitch-fork's prongs:
Slowly bright objects formed when you went in.
Then you felt cobwebs clogging up your lungs

And scuttled fast into the sunlit yard –
And into nights when bats were on the wing
Over the rafters of sleep, where bright eyes stared
From piles of grain in corners, fierce, unblinking.

The dark gulfed like a roof-space. I was chaff
To be pecked up when birds shot through the air-slits.
I lay face-down to shun the fear above.
The two-lugged sacks moved in like great blind rats.

An Advancement of Learning

I took the embankment path
(As always, deferring
The bridge). The river nosed past,
Pliable, oil-skinned, wearing

A transfer of gables and sky.
Hunched over the railing,
Well away from the road now, I
Considered the dirty-keeled swans.

Something slobbered curtly, close,
Smudging the silence: a rat
Slimed out of the water and
My throat sickened so quickly that

I turned down the path in cold sweat
But God, another was nimbling
Up the far bank, tracing its wet
Arcs on the stones. Incredibly then

I established a dreaded
Bridgehead. I turned to stare
With deliberate, thrilled care
At my hitherto snubbed rodent.

He clockworked aimlessly a while,
Stopped, back bunched and glistening,
Ears plastered down on his knobbled skull,
Insidiously listening.

The tapered tail that followed him,
The raindrop eye, the old snout:
One by one I took all in.
He trained on me. I stared him out

Forgetting how I used to panic
When his grey brothers scraped and fed
Behind the hen-coop in our yard,
On ceiling boards above my bed.

This terror, cold, wet-furred, small-clawed,
Retreated up a pipe for sewage.
I stared a minute after him.
Then I walked on and crossed the bridge.

Blackberry-Picking

For Philip Hobsbaum

Late August, given heavy rain and sun
For a full week, the blackberries would ripen.
At first, just one, a glossy purple clot
Among others, red, green, hard as a knot.
You ate that first one and its flesh was sweet
Like thickened wine: summer's blood was in it
Leaving stains upon the tongue and lust for
Picking. Then red ones inked up, and that hunger
Sent us out with milk-cans, pea-tins, jam-pots
Where briars scratched and wet grass bleached our boots.
Round hayfields, cornfields and potato-drills,
We trekked and picked until the cans were full,
Until the tinkling bottom had been covered
With green ones, and on top big dark blobs burned
Like a plate of eyes. Our hands were peppered
With thorn pricks, our palms sticky as Bluebeard's.

We hoarded the fresh berries in the byre.
But when the bath was filled we found a fur,
A rat-grey fungus, glutting on our cache.
The juice was stinking too. Once off the bush,
The fruit fermented, the sweet flesh would turn sour.
I always felt like crying. It wasn't fair
That all the lovely canfuls smelt of rot.
Each year I hoped they'd keep, knew they would not.

Churning Day

A thick crust, coarse-grained as limestone rough-cast,
hardened gradually on top of the four crocks
that stood, large pottery bombs, in the small pantry.
After the hot brewery of gland, cud and udder,
cool porous earthenware fermented the buttermilk
for churning day, when the hooped churn was scoured
with plumping kettles and the busy scrubber
echoed daintily on the seasoned wood.
It stood then, purified, on the flagged kitchen floor.

Out came the four crocks, spilled their heavy lip
of cream, their white insides, into the sterile churn.
The staff, like a great whisky muddler fashioned
in deal wood, was plunged in, the lid fitted.
My mother took first turn, set up rhythms
that slugged and thumped for hours. Arms ached.
Hands blistered. Cheeks and clothes were spattered

with flabby milk.
                         Where finally gold flecks
began to dance. They poured hot water then,
sterilized a birchwood-bowl
and little corrugated butter-spades.
Their short stroke quickened, suddenly
a yellow curd was weighting the churned up white,
heavy and rich, coagulated sunlight
that they fished, dripping, in a wide tin strainer,
heaped up like gilded gravel in the bowl.

The house would stink long after churning day,
acrid as a sulphur mine. The empty crocks
were ranged along the wall again, the butter
in soft printed slabs was piled on pantry shelves.
And in the house we moved with gravid ease,

our brains turned crystals full of clean deal churns,
the plash and gurgle of the sour-breathed milk,
the pat and slap of small spades on wet lumps.

The Early Purges

I was six when I first saw kittens drown.
Dan Taggart pitched them, 'the scraggy wee shits',
Into a bucket; a frail metal sound,

Soft paws scraping like mad. But their tiny din
Was soon soused. They were slung on the snout
Of the pump and the water pumped in.

'Sure isn't it better for them now?' Dan said.
Like wet gloves they bobbed and shone till he sluiced
Them out on the dunghill, glossy and dead.

Suddenly frightened, for days I sadly hung
Round the yard, watching the three sogged remains
Turn mealy and crisp as old summer dung

Until I forgot them. But the fear came back
When Dan trapped big rats, snared rabbits, shot crows
Or, with a sickening tug, pulled old hens' necks.

Still, living displaces false sentiments
And now, when shrill pups are prodded to drown,
I just shrug, 'Bloody pups'. It makes sense:

'Prevention of cruelty' talk cuts ice in town
Where they consider death unnatural,
But on well-run farms pests have to be kept down.

Follower

My father worked with a horse-plough,
His shoulders globed like a full sail strung
Between the shafts and the furrow.
The horses strained at his clicking tongue.

An expert. He would set the wing
And fit the bright steel-pointed sock.
The sod rolled over without breaking.
At the headrig, with a single pluck

Of reins, the sweating team turned round
And back into the land. His eye
Narrowed and angled at the ground,
Mapping the furrow exactly.

I stumbled in his hob-nailed wake,
Fell sometimes on the polished sod;
Sometimes he rode me on his back,
Dipping and rising to his plod.

I wanted to grow up and plough,
To close one eye, stiffen my arm.
All I ever did was follow
In his broad shadow round the farm.

I was a nuisance, tripping, falling,
Yapping always. But today
It is my father who keeps stumbling
Behind me, and will not go away.

Ancestral Photograph

Jaws puff round and solid as a turnip,
Dead eyes are statue's and the upper lip
Bullies the heavy mouth down to a droop.
A bowler suggests the stage Irishman
Whose look has two parts scorn, two parts dead pan.
His silver watch chain girds him like a hoop.

My father's uncle, from whom he learnt the trade,
Long fixed in sepia tints, begins to fade
And must come down. Now on the bedroom wall
There is a faded patch where he has been –
As if a bandage had been ripped from skin –
Empty plaque to a house's rise and fall.

Twenty years ago I herded cattle
Into pens or held them against a wall
Until my father won at arguing
His own price on a crowd of cattlemen
Who handled rumps, groped teats, stood, paused and then
Bought a round of drinks to clinch the bargain.

Uncle and nephew, fifty years ago,
Heckled and herded through the fair days too.
This barrel of a man penned in the frame:
I see him with the jaunty hat pushed back
Draw thumbs out of his waistcoat, curtly smack
Hands and sell. Father, I've watched you do the same

And watched you sadden when the fairs were stopped.
No room for dealers if the farmers shopped
Like housewives at an auction ring. Your stick
Was parked behind the door and stands there still.
Closing this chapter of our chronicle,
I take your uncle's portrait to the attic.

Mid-Term Break

I sat all morning in the college sick bay,
Counting bells knelling classes to a close.
At two o'clock our neighbours drove me home.

In the porch I met my father crying –
He had always taken funerals in his stride –
And Big Jim Evans saying it was a hard blow.

The baby cooed and laughed and rocked the pram
When I came in, and I was embarrassed
By old men standing up to shake my hand

And tell me they were 'sorry for my trouble'.
Whispers informed strangers I was the eldest,
Away at school, as my mother held my hand

In hers and coughed out angry tearless sighs.
At ten o'clock the ambulance arrived
With the corpse, stanched and bandaged by the nurses.

Next morning I went up into the room. Snowdrops
And candles soothed the bedside; I saw him
For the first time in six weeks. Paler now,

Wearing a poppy bruise on his left temple,
He lay in the four foot box as in his cot.
No gaudy scars, the bumper knocked him clear.

A four foot box, a foot for every year.

Dawn Shoot

Clouds ran their wet mortar, plastered the daybreak
Grey. The stones clicked tartly
If we missed the sleepers, but mostly
Silent we headed up the railway
Where now the only steam was funnelling from cows
Ditched on their rumps beyond hedges,
Cudding, watching, and knowing.
The rails scored a bull's-eye into the eye
Of a bridge. A corncrake challenged
Unexpectedly like a hoarse sentry
And a snipe rocketed away on reconnaissance.
Rubber-booted, belted, tense as two parachutists,
We climbed the iron gate and dropped
Into the meadow's six acres of broom, gorse and dew.

A sandy bank, reinforced with coiling roots,
Faced you, two hundred yards from the track.
Snug on our bellies behind a rise of dead whins,
Our ravenous eyes getting used to the greyness,
We settled, soon had the holes under cover.
This was the den they all would be heading for now,
Loping under ferns in dry drains, flashing
Brown orbits across ploughlands and grazing.

The plaster thinned at the skyline, the whitewash
Was bleaching on houses and stables,
The cock would be sounding reveille
In seconds.
And there was one breaking
In from the gap in the corner.

Donnelly's left hand came up
And came down on my barrel. This one was his,
'For Christ's sake,' I spat, 'Take your time, there'll

be more.'
There was the playboy trotting up to the hole
By the ash tree, 'Wild rover no more,'
Said Donnelly and emptied two barrels
And got him.

Another snipe catapulted into the light,
A mare whinnied and shivered her haunches
Up on a hill. The others would not be back
After three shots like that. We dandered off
To the railway; the prices were small at that time
So we did not bother to cut out the tongue.
The ones that slipped back when the all clear got round
Would be first to examine him.

At a Potato Digging

A mechanical digger wrecks the drill,
Spins up a dark shower of roots and mould.
Labourers swarm in behind, stoop to fill
Wicker creels. Fingers go dead in the cold.

Like crows attacking crow-black fields, they stretch
A higgledy line from hedge to headland;
Some pairs keep breaking ragged ranks to fetch
A full creel to the pit and straighten, stand

Tall for a moment but soon stumble back
To fish a new load from the crumbled surf.
Heads bow, trunks bend, hands fumble towards the black
Mother. Processional stooping through the turf

Recurs mindlessly as autumn. Centuries
Of fear and homage to the famine god
Toughen the muscles behind their humbled knees,
Make a seasonal altar of the sod.

II

Flint-white, purple. They lie scattered
like inflated pebbles. Native
to the black hutch of clay
where the halved seed shot and clotted,
these knobbed and slit-eyed tubers seem
the petrified hearts of drills. Split
by the spade, they show white as cream.

Good smells exude from crumbled earth.
The rough bark of humus erupts
knots of potatoes (a clean birth)

whose solid feel, whose wet insides
promise taste of ground and root.
To be piled in pits; live skulls, blind-eyed.

III

Live skulls, blind-eyed, balanced on
wild higgledy skeletons,
scoured the land in 'forty-five,
wolfed the blighted root and died.

The new potato, sound as stone,
putrefied when it had lain
three days in the long clay pit.
Millions rotted along with it.

Mouths tightened in, eyes died hard,
faces chilled to a plucked bird.
In a million wicker huts,
beaks of famine snipped at guts.

A people hungering from birth,
grubbing, like plants, in the earth,
were grafted with a great sorrow.
Hope rotted like a marrow.

Stinking potatoes fouled the land,
pits turned pus into filthy mounds:
and where potato diggers are,
you still smell the running sore.

IV

Under a gay flotilla of gulls
The rhythm deadens, the workers stop.
Brown bread and tea in bright canfuls
Are served for lunch. Dead-beat, they flop

Down in the ditch and take their fill,
Thankfully breaking timeless fasts;
Then, stretched on the faithless ground, spill
Libations of cold tea, scatter crusts.

For the Commander of the 'Eliza'

...the others, with emaciated faces and prominent, staring eyeballs, were evidently in an advanced state of starvation. The officer reported to Sir James Dombrain... and Sir James, 'very inconveniently', wrote Routh, 'interfered'.
        CECIL WOODHAM-SMITH: THE GREAT HUNGER

Routine patrol off West Mayo; sighting
A rowboat heading unusually far
Beyond the creek, I tacked and hailed the crew
In Gaelic. Their stroke had clearly weakened
As they pulled to, from guilt or bashfulness
I was conjecturing when, O my sweet Christ,
We saw piled in the bottom of their craft
Six grown men with gaping mouths and eyes
Bursting the sockets like spring onions in drills.
Six wrecks of bone and pallid, tautened skin.
'Bia, bia,
Bia'. In whines and snarls their desperation
Rose and fell like a flock of starving gulls.
We'd known about the shortage, but on board
They always kept us right with flour and beef
So understand my feelings, and the men's,
Who had no mandate to relieve distress
Since relief was then available in Westport –
Though clearly these poor brutes would never make it.
I had to refuse food: they cursed and howled
Like dogs that had been kicked hard in the privates.
When they drove at me with their starboard oar
(Risking capsize themselves) I saw they were
Violent and without hope. I hoisted
And cleared off. Less incidents the better.
Next day, like six bad smells, those living skulls
Drifted through the dark of bunks and hatches
And once in port I exorcised my ship,
Reporting all to the Inspector General.

Sir James, I understand, urged free relief
For famine victims in the Westport Sector
And earned tart reprimand from good Whitehall.
Let natives prosper by their own exertions;
Who could not swim might go ahead and sink.
'The Coast Guard with their zeal and activity
Are too lavish' were the words, I think.

The Diviner

Cut from the green hedge a forked hazel stick
That he held tight by the arms of the V:
Circling the terrain, hunting the pluck
Of water, nervous, but professionally

Unfussed. The pluck came sharp as a sting.
The rod jerked with precise convulsions,
Spring water suddenly broadcasting
Through a green hazel its secret stations.

The bystanders would ask to have a try.
He handed them the rod without a word.
It lay dead in their grasp till, nonchalantly,
He gripped expectant wrists. The hazel stirred.

Turkeys Observed

One observes them, one expects them;
Blue-breasted in their indifferent mortuary,
Beached bare on the cold marble slabs
In immodest underwear frills of feather.

The red sides of beef retain
Some of the smelly majesty of living:
A half-cow slung from a hook maintains
That blood and flesh are not ignored.

But a turkey cowers in death.
Pull his neck, pluck him, and look –
He is just another poor forked thing,
A skin bag plumped with inky putty.

He once complained extravagantly
In an overture of gobbles;
He lorded it on the claw-flecked mud
With a grey flick of his Confucian eye.

Now, as I pass the bleak Christmas dazzle,
I find him ranged with his cold squadrons:
The fuselage is bare, the proud wings snapped,
The tail-fan stripped down to a shameful rudder.

Cow in Calf

It seems she has swallowed a barrel.
From forelegs to haunches,
her belly is slung like a hammock.

Slapping her out of the byre is like slapping
a great bag of seed. My hand
tingled as if strapped, but I had to
hit her again and again and
heard the blows plump like a depth-charge
far in her gut.

The udder grows. Windbags
of bagpipes are crammed there
to drone in her lowing.
Her cud and her milk, her heats and her calves
keep coming and going.

Trout

Hangs, a fat gun-barrel,
deep under arched bridges
or slips like butter down
the throat of the river.

From depths smooth-skinned as plums,
his muzzle gets bull's eye;
picks off grass-seed and moths
that vanish, torpedoed.

Where water unravels
over gravel-beds he
is fired from the shallows,
white belly reporting

flat; darts like a tracer-
bullet back between stones
and is never burnt out.
A volley of cold blood

ramrodding the current.

Waterfall

The burn drowns steadily in its own downpour,
A helter-skelter of muslin and glass
That skids to a halt, crashing up suds.

Simultaneous acceleration
And sudden braking; water goes over
Like villains dropped screaming to justice.

It appears an athletic glacier
Has reared into reverse: is swallowed up
And regurgitated through this long throat.

My eye rides over and downwards, falls with
Hurtling tons that slabber and spill,
Falls, yet records the tumult thus standing still.

Docker

There, in the corner, staring at his drink.
The cap juts like a gantry's crossbeam,
Cowling plated forehead and sledgehead jaw.
Speech is clamped in the lips' vice.

That fist would drop a hammer on a Catholic –
Oh yes, that kind of thing could start again.
The only Roman collar he tolerates
Smiles all round his sleek pint of porter.

Mosaic imperatives bang home like rivets;
God is a foreman with certain definite views
Who orders life in shifts of work and leisure.
A factory horn will blare the Resurrection.

He sits, strong and blunt as a Celtic cross,
Clearly used to silence and an armchair:
Tonight the wife and children will be quiet
At slammed door and smoker's cough in the hall.

Poor Women in a City Church

The small wax candles melt to light,
Flicker in marble, reflect bright
Asterisks on brass candlesticks:
At the Virgin's altar on the right,
Blue flames are jerking on wicks.

Old dough-faced women with black shawls
Drawn down tight kneel in the stalls.
Cold yellow candle-tongues, blue flame
Mince and caper as whispered calls
Take wing up to the Holy Name.

Thus each day in the sacred place
They kneel. Golden shrines, altar lace,
Marble columns and cool shadows
Still them. In the gloom you cannot trace
A wrinkle on their beeswax brows.

Gravities

High-riding kites appear to range quite freely,
Though reined by strings, strict and invisible.
The pigeon that deserts you suddenly
Is heading home, instinctively faithful.

Lovers with barrages of hot insult
Often cut off their nose to spite their face,
Endure a hopeless day, declare their guilt,
Re-enter the native port of their embrace.

Blinding in Paris, for his party-piece
Joyce named the shops along O'Connell Street
And on Iona Colmcille sought ease
By wearing Irish mould next to his feet.

Twice Shy

Her scarf *à la* Bardot,
In suede flats for the walk,
She came with me one evening
For air and friendly talk.
We crossed the quiet river,
Took the embankment walk.

Traffic holding its breath,
Sky a tense diaphragm:
Dusk hung like a backcloth
That shook where a swan swam,
Tremulous as a hawk
Hanging deadly, calm.

A vacuum of need
Collapsed each hunting heart
But tremulously we held
As hawk and prey apart,
Preserved classic decorum,
Deployed our talk with art.

Our juvenilia
Had taught us both to wait,
Not to publish feeling
And regret it all too late –
Mushroom loves already
Had puffed and burst in hate.

So, chary and excited
As a thrush linked on a hawk,
We thrilled to the March twilight
With nervous childish talk:
Still waters running deep
Along the embankment walk.

Valediction

Lady with the frilled blouse
And simple tartan skirt,
Since you left the house
Its emptiness has hurt
All thought. In your presence
Time rode easy, anchored
On a smile; but absence
Rocked love's balance, unmoored
The days. They buck and bound
Across the calendar,
Pitched from the quiet sound
Of your flower-tender
Voice. Need breaks on my strand;
You've gone, I am at sea.
Until you resume command,
Self is in mutiny.

Lovers on Aran

The timeless waves, bright, sifting, broken glass,
Came dazzling around, into the rocks,
Came glinting, sifting from the Americas

To possess Aran. Or did Aran rush
To throw wide arms of rock around a tide
That yielded with an ebb, with a soft crash?

Did sea define the land or land the sea?
Each drew new meaning from the waves' collision.
Sea broke on land to full identity.

Poem

For Marie

Love, I shall perfect for you the child
Who diligently potters in my brain
Digging with heavy spade till sods were piled
Or puddling through muck in a deep drain.

Yearly I would sow my yard-long garden.
I'd strip a layer of sods to build the wall
That was to exclude sow and pecking hen.
Yearly, admitting these, the sods would fall.

Or in the sucking clabber I would splash
Delightedly and dam the flowing drain,
But always my bastions of clay and mush
Would burst before the rising autumn rain.

Love, you shall perfect for me this child
Whose small imperfect limits would keep breaking:
Within new limits now, arrange the world
Within our walls, within our golden ring.

Honeymoon Flight

Below, the patchwork earth, dark hems of hedge,
The long grey tapes of road that bind and loose
Villages and fields in casual marriage:
We bank above the small lough and farmhouse

And the sure green world goes topsy-turvy
As we climb out of our familiar landscape.
The engine noises change. You look at me.
The coastline slips away beneath the wing-tip.

And launched right off the earth by force of fire,
We hang, miraculous, above the water,
Dependent on the invisible air
To keep us airborne and to bring us further.

Ahead of us the sky's a geyser now.
A calm voice talks of cloud yet we feel lost.
Air-pockets jolt our fears and down we go.
Travellers, at this point, can only trust.

Scaffolding

Masons, when they start upon a building,
Are careful to test out the scaffolding;

Make sure that planks won't slip at busy points,
Secure all ladders, tighten bolted joints.

And yet all this comes down when the job's done,
Showing off walls of sure and solid stone.

So if, my dear, there sometimes seem to be
Old bridges breaking between you and me,

Never fear. We may let the scaffolds fall,
Confident that we have built our wall.

Storm on the Island

We are prepared: we build our houses squat,
Sink walls in rock and roof them with good slate.
This wizened earth has never troubled us
With hay, so, as you see, there are no stacks
Or stooks that can be lost. Nor are there trees
Which might prove company when it blows full
Blast: you know what I mean – leaves and branches
Can raise a tragic chorus in a gale
So that you listen to the thing you fear
Forgetting that it pummels your house too.
But there are no trees, no natural shelter.
You might think that the sea is company,
Exploding comfortably down on the cliffs,
But no: when it begins, the flung spray hits
The very windows, spits like a tame cat
Turned savage. We just sit tight while wind dives
And strafes invisibly. Space is a salvo,
We are bombarded by the empty air.
Strange, it is a huge nothing that we fear.

Synge on Aran

Salt off the sea whets
the blades of four winds.
They peel acres
of locked rock, pare down
a rind of shrivelled ground;
bull-noses are chiselled
on cliffs.
       Islanders too
are for sculpting. Note
the pointed scowl, the mouth
carved as upturned anchor
and the polished head
full of drownings.
             There
he comes now, a hard pen
scraping in his head;
the nib filed on a salt wind
and dipped in the keening sea.

Saint Francis and the Birds

When Francis preached love to the birds,
They listened, fluttered, throttled up
Into the blue like a flock of words

Released for fun from his holy lips.
Then wheeled back, whirred about his head,
Pirouetted on brothers' capes,

Danced on the wing, for sheer joy played
And sang, like images took flight.
Which was the best poem Francis made,

His argument true, his tone light.

In Small Townlands

For Colin Middleton

In small townlands his hogshair wedge
Will split the granite from the clay
Till crystal in the rock is bared:
Loaded brushes hone an edge
On mountain blue and heather grey.
Outcrops of stone contract, outstared.

The spectrum bursts, a bright grenade,
When he unlocks the safety catch
On morning dew, on cloud, on rain.
The splintered lights slice like a spade
That strips the land of fuzz and blotch,
Pares clean as bone, cruel as the pain

That strikes in a wild heart attack.
His eyes, thick, greedy lenses, fire
This bare bald earth with white and red,
Incinerate it till it's black
And brilliant as a funeral pyre:
A new world cools out of his head.

The Folk Singers

Re-turning time-turned words,
Fitting each weathered song
To a new-grooved harmony,
They pluck slick strings and swing
A sad heart's equilibrium.

Numb passion, pearled in the shy
Shell of a country love
And strung on a frail tune,
Looks sharp now, strikes a pose
Like any rustic new to the bright town.

Their pre-packed tale will sell
Ten thousand times: pale love
Rouged for the streets. Humming
Solders all broken hearts. Death's edge
Blunts on the narcotic strumming.

The Play Way

Sunlight pillars through glass, probes each desk
For milk-tops, drinking straws and old dry crusts.
The music strides to challenge it,
Mixing memory and desire with chalk dust.

My lesson notes read: *Teacher will play*
Beethoven's Concerto Number Five
And class will express themselves freely
In writing. One said 'Can we jive?'

When I produced the record, but now
The big sound has silenced them. Higher
And firmer, each authoritative note
Pumps the classroom up tight as a tyre,

Working its private spell behind eyes
That stare wide. They have forgotten me
For once. The pens are busy, the tongues mime
Their blundering embrace of the free

Word. A silence charged with sweetness
Breaks short on lost faces where I see
New looks. Then notes stretch taut as snares. They
trip
To fall into themselves unknowingly.

Personal Helicon

For Michael Longley

As a child, they could not keep me from wells
And old pumps with buckets and windlasses.
I loved the dark drop, the trapped sky, the smells
Of waterweed, fungus and dank moss.

One, in a brickyard, with a rotted board top.
I savoured the rich crash when a bucket
Plummeted down at the end of a rope.
So deep you saw no reflection in it.

A shallow one under a dry stone ditch
Fructified like any aquarium.
When you dragged out long roots from the soft mulch,
A white face hovered over the bottom.

Others had echoes, gave back your own call
With a clean new music in it. And one
Was scaresome for there, out of ferns and tall
Foxgloves, a rat slapped across my reflection.

Now, to pry into roots, to finger slime,
To stare, big-eyed Narcissus, into some spring
Is beneath all adult dignity. I rhyme
To see myself, to set the darkness echoing.

Door into the Dark

For my father and mother

Contents

Acknowledgements

Acknowledgements are due to the editors of the following magazines, in which some of these poems have appeared:

The Dublin Magazine, The Honest Ulsterman, The Irish Press, The Irish Times, The Listener, New Statesman, Outposts, Phoenix, Times Literary Supplement, University Review; and to the Northern Ireland Service of the BBC. Some details in "Requiem for the Croppies" are taken from P. O'Kelly's *General History of the Rebellion of 1798*, Dublin, 1842.

Night-Piece

Must you know it again?
Dull pounding through hay,
The uneasy whinny.

A sponge lip drawn off each separate tooth.
Opalescent haunch,
Muscle and hoof

Bundled under the roof.

Gone

Green froth that lathered each end
Of the shining bit
Is a cobweb of grass-dust.
The sweaty twist of the bellyband
Has stiffened, cold in the hand,
And pads of the blinkers
Bulge through the ticking.
Reins, chains and traces
Droop in a tangle.

His hot reek is lost.
The place is old in his must.

He cleared in a hurry
Clad only in shods
Leaving this stable unmade.

Dream

With a billhook
Whose head was hand-forged and heavy
I was hacking a stalk
Thick as a telegraph pole.
My sleeves were rolled
And the air fanned cool past my arms
As I swung and buried the blade,
Then laboured to work it unstuck.

The next stroke
Found a man's head under the hook.
Before I woke
I heard the steel stop
In the bone of the brow.

The Outlaw

Kelly's kept an unlicensed bull, well away
From the road: you risked a fine but had to pay

The normal fee if cows were serviced there.
Once I dragged a nervous Friesian on a tether

Down a lane of alder, shaggy with catkin,
Down to the shed the bull was kept in.

I gave Old Kelly the clammy silver, though why
I could not guess. He grunted a curt 'Go by.

Get up on that gate.' And from my lofty station
I watched the business-like conception.

The door, unbolted, whacked back against the wall.
The illegal sire fumbled from his stall

Unhurried as an old steam-engine shunting.
He circled, snored and nosed. No hectic panting,

Just the unfussy ease of a good tradesman;
Then an awkward, unexpected jump, and,

His knobbled forelegs straddling her flank,
He slammed life home, impassive as a tank,

Dropping off like a tipped-up load of sand.
'She'll do,' said Kelly and tapped his ash-plant

Across her hindquarters. 'If not, bring her back.'
I walked ahead of her, the rope now slack,

While Kelly whooped and prodded his outlaw
Who, in his own time, resumed the dark, the straw.

The Salmon Fisher to the Salmon

The ridged lip set upstream, you flail
Inland again, your exile in the sea
Unconditionally cancelled by the pull
    Of your home water's gravity.

And I stand in the centre, casting.
The river cramming under me reflects
Slung gaff and net and a white wrist flicking
    Flies well-dressed with tint and fleck.

Walton thought garden worms, perfumed
By oil crushed from dark ivy berries
The lure that took you best, but here you come
    To grief through hunger in your eyes.

Ripples arrowing beyond me,
The current strumming water up my leg,
Involved in water's choreography
    I go, like you, by gleam and drag

And will strike when you strike, to kill.
We're both annihilated on the fly.
You can't resist a gullet full of steel.
    I will turn home, fish-smelling, scaly.

The Forge

All I know is a door into the dark.
Outside, old axles and iron hoops rusting;
Inside, the hammered anvil's short-pitched ring,
The unpredictable fantail of sparks
Or hiss when a new shoe toughens in water.
The anvil must be somewhere in the centre,
Horned as a unicorn, at one end square,
Set there immovable: an altar
Where he expends himself in shape and music.
Sometimes, leather-aproned, hairs in his nose,
He leans out on the jamb, recalls a clatter
Of hoofs where traffic is flashing in rows;
Then grunts and goes in, with a slam and flick
To beat real iron out, to work the bellows.

Thatcher

Bespoke for weeks, he turned up some morning
Unexpectedly, his bicycle slung
With a light ladder and a bag of knives.
He eyed the old rigging, poked at the eaves,

Opened and handled sheaves of lashed wheat-straw.
Next, the bundled rods: hazel and willow
Were flicked for weight, twisted in case they'd snap.
It seemed he spent the morning warming up:

Then fixed the ladder, laid out well-honed blades
And snipped at straw and sharpened ends of rods
That, bent in two, made a white-pronged staple
For pinning down his world, handful by handful.

Couchant for days on sods above the rafters,
He shaved and flushed the butts, stitched all together
Into a sloped honeycomb, a stubble patch,
And left them gaping at his Midas touch.

The Peninsula

When you have nothing more to say, just drive
For a day all round the peninsula.
The sky is tall as over a runway,
The land without marks so you will not arrive

But pass through, though always skirting landfall.
At dusk, horizons drink down sea and hill,
The ploughed field swallows the whitewashed gable
And you're in the dark again. Now recall

The glazed foreshore and silhouetted log,
That rock where breakers shredded into rags,
The leggy birds stilted on their own legs,
Islands riding themselves out into the fog

And drive back home, still with nothing to say
Except that now you will uncode all landscapes
By this: things founded clean on their own shapes,
Water and ground in their extremity.

In Gallarus Oratory

You can still feel the community pack
This place: it's like going into a turfstack,
A core of old dark walled up with stone
A yard thick. When you're in it alone,
You might have dropped, a reduced creature,
To the heart of the globe. No worshipper
Would leap up to his God off this floor.

Founded there like heroes in a barrow,
They sought themselves in the eye of their King
Under the black weight of their own breathing.
And how he smiled on them as out they came,
The sea a censer and the grass a flame.

Girls Bathing, Galway, 1965

The swell foams where they float and crawl,
A catherine-wheel of arm and hand;
Each head bobs curtly as a football.
The yelps are faint here on the strand.

No milk-limbed Venus ever rose
Miraculous on this western shore.
A pirate queen in battle clothes
Is our sterner myth. The breakers pour

Themselves into themselves, the years
Shuttle through space invisibly.
Where crests unfurl like creamy beer
The queen's clothes melt into the sea

And generations sighing in
The salt suds where the wave has crashed
Labour in fear of flesh and sin
For the time has been accomplished

As through the shallows in swimsuits,
Bare-legged, smooth-shouldered and long-backed,
They wade ashore with skips and shouts.
So Venus comes, matter-of-fact.

Requiem for the Croppies

The pockets of our greatcoats full of barley –
No kitchens on the run, no striking camp –
We moved quick and sudden in our own country.
The priest lay behind ditches with the tramp.
A people, hardly marching – on the hike –
We found new tactics happening each day:
We'd cut through reins and rider with the pike
And stampede cattle into infantry,
Then retreat through hedges where cavalry must be thrown.
Until, on Vinegar Hill, the fatal conclave.
Terraced thousands died, shaking scythes at cannon.
The hillside blushed, soaked in our broken wave.
They buried us without shroud or coffin
And in August the barley grew up out of the grave.

Rite of Spring

So winter closed its fist
And got it stuck in the pump.
The plunger froze up a lump

In its throat, ice founding itself
Upon iron. The handle
Paralysed at an angle.

Then the twisting of wheat straw
Into ropes, lapping them tight
Round stem and snout, then a light

That sent the pump up in flame.
It cooled, we lifted her latch,
Her entrance was wet, and she came.

Undine

He slashed the briars, shovelled up grey silt
To give me right of way in my own drains
And I ran quick for him, cleaned out my rust.

He halted, saw me finally disrobed,
Running clear, with apparent unconcern.
Then he walked by me. I rippled and I churned

Where ditches intersected near the river
Until he dug a spade deep in my flank
And took me to him. I swallowed his trench

Gratefully, dispersing myself for love
Down in his roots, climbing his brassy grain –
But once he knew my welcome, I alone

Could give him subtle increase and reflection.
He explored me so completely, each limb
Lost its cold freedom. Human, warmed to him.

The Wife's Tale

When I had spread it all on linen cloth
Under the hedge, I called them over.
The hum and gulp of the thresher ran down
And the big belt slewed to a standstill, straw
Hanging undelivered in the jaws.
There was such quiet that I heard their boots
Crunching the stubble twenty yards away.

He lay down and said 'Give these fellows theirs,
I'm in no hurry,' plucking grass in handfuls
And tossing it in the air. 'That looks well.'
(He nodded at my white cloth on the grass.)
'I declare a woman could lay out a field
Though boys like us have little call for cloths.'
He winked, then watched me as I poured a cup
And buttered the thick slices that he likes.
'It's threshing better than I thought, and mind
It's good clean seed. Away over there and look.'
Always this inspection has to be made
Even when I don't know what to look for.

But I ran my hand in the half-filled bags
Hooked to the slots. It was hard as shot,
Innumerable and cool. The bags gaped
Where the chutes ran back to the stilled drum
And forks were stuck at angles in the ground
As javelins might mark lost battlefields.
I moved between them back across the stubble.
They lay in the ring of their own crusts and dregs
Smoking and saying nothing. 'There's good yield,
Isn't there?' – as proud as if he were the land itself –
'Enough for crushing and for sowing both.'
And that was it. I'd come and he had shown me
So I belonged no further to the work.

I gathered cups and folded up the cloth
And went. But they still kept their ease
Spread out, unbuttoned, grateful, under the trees.

Mother

As I work at the pump, the wind heavy
With spits of rain is fraying
The rope of water I'm pumping.
It pays itself out like air's afterbirth
At each gulp of the plunger.

I am tired of the feeding of stock.
Each evening I labour this handle
Half an hour at a time, the cows
Guzzling at bowls in the byre.
Before I have topped up the level
They lower it down.

They've trailed in again by the ready-made gate
He stuck into the fence: a jingling bedhead
Wired up between posts. It's on its last legs.
It does not jingle for joy any more.

I am tired of walking about with this plunger
Inside me. God, he plays like a young calf
Gone wild on a rope.
Lying or standing won't settle these capers,
This gulp in my well.

O when I am a gate for myself
Let such wind fray my waters
As scarfs my skirt through my thighs,
Stuffs air down my throat.

Cana Revisited

No round-shouldered pitchers here, no stewards
To supervise consumption or supplies
And water locked behind the taps implies
No expectation of miraculous words.

But in the bone-hooped womb, rising like yeast,
Virtue intact is waiting to be shown,
The consecration wondrous (being their own)
As when the water reddened at the feast.

Elegy for a Still-born Child

I

Your mother walks light as an empty creel
Unlearning the intimate nudge and pull

Your trussed-up weight of seed-flesh and bone-curd
Had insisted on. That evicted world

Contracts round its history, its scar.
Doomsday struck when your collapsed sphere

Extinguished itself in our atmosphere,
Your mother heavy with the lightness in her.

II

For six months you stayed cartographer,
Charting my friend from husband towards father.

He guessed a globe behind your steady mound.
Then the pole fell, shooting star, into the ground.

III

On lonely journeys I think of it all,
Birth of death, exhumation for burial,

A wreath of small clothes, a memorial pram,
And parents reaching for a phantom limb.

I drive by remote control on this bare road
Under a drizzling sky, a circling rook,

Past mountain fields, full to the brim with cloud,
White waves riding home on a wintry lough.

Victorian Guitar

For David Hammond

Inscribed 'Belonged to Louisa Catherine Coe before her marriage to John Charles Smith, March 1852.'

I expected the lettering to carry
The date of the gift, a kind of christening:
This is more like the plate on a coffin.

Louisa Catherine Smith could not be light.
Far more than a maiden name
Was cancelled by him on the first night.

I believe he cannot have known your touch
Like this instrument – for clearly
John Charles did not hold with fingering –

Which is obviously a lady's:
The sound-box trim as a girl in stays,
The neck right for the smallest span.

Did you even keep track of it as a wife?
Do you know the man who has it now
Is giving it the time of its life?

Night Drive

The smells of ordinariness
Were new on the night drive through France:
Rain and hay and woods on the air
Made warm draughts in the open car.

Signposts whitened relentlessly.
Montreuil, Abbéville, Beauvais
Were promised, promised, came and went,
Each place granting its name's fulfilment.

A combine groaning its way late
Bled seeds across its work-light.
A forest fire smouldered out.
One by one small cafés shut.

I thought of you continuously
A thousand miles south where Italy
Laid its loin to France on the darkened sphere.
Your ordinariness was renewed there.

At Ardboe Point

Right along the lough shore
A smoke of flies
Drifts thick in the sunset.

They come shattering daintily
Against the windscreen,
The grill and bonnet whisper

At their million collisions:
It is to drive through
A hail of fine chaff.

Yet we leave no clear wake
For they open and close on us
As the air opens and closes.

Tonight when we put out our light
To kiss between sheets
Their just audible siren will go

Outside the window,
Their invisible veil
Weakening the moonlight still further,

And the walls will carry a rash
Of them, a green pollen.
They'll have infiltrated our clothes by morning.

If you put one under a lens
You'd be looking at a pumping body
With such outsize beaters for wings

That this visitation would seem
More drastic than Pharaoh's.

I'm told they're mosquitoes

But I'd need forests and swamps
To believe it
For these are our innocent, shuttling

Choirs, dying through
Their own live empyrean, troublesome only
As the last veil on a dancer.

Relic of Memory

The lough waters
Can petrify wood:
Old oars and posts
Over the years
Harden their grain,
Incarcerate ghosts

Of sap and season.
The shallows lap
And give and take:
Constant ablutions,
Such drowning love
Stun a stake

To stalagmite.
Dead lava,
The cooling star,
Coal and diamond
Or sudden birth
Of burnt meteor

Are too simple,
Without the lure
That relic stored –
A piece of stone
On the shelf at school,
Oatmeal coloured.

A Lough Neagh Sequence

For the fishermen

1. *Up the Shore*

I

The lough will claim a victim every year.
It has virtue that hardens wood to stone.
There is a town sunk beneath its water.
It is the scar left by the Isle of Man.

II

At Toomebridge where it sluices towards the sea
They've set new gates and tanks against the flow.
From time to time they break the eels' journey
And lift five hundred stones in one go.

III

But up the shore in Antrim and Tyrone
There is a sense of fair play in the game.
The fishermen confront them one by one
And sail miles out and never learn to swim.

IV

'We'll be the quicker going down,' they say.
And when you argue there are no storms here,
That one hour floating's sure to land them safely –
'The lough will claim a victim every year.'

2. *Beyond Sargasso*

A gland agitating
mud two hundred miles in-
land, a scale of water
on water working up
estuaries, he drifted
into motion half-way
across the Atlantic,
sure as the satellite's
insinuating pull
in the ocean, as true
to his orbit.
     Against
ebb, current, rock, rapids,
a muscled icicle
that melts itself longer
and fatter, he buries
his arrival beyond
light and tidal water,
investing silt and sand
with a sleek root. By day,
only the drainmaker's
spade or the mud paddler
can make him abort. Dark
delivers him hungering
down each undulation.

3. *Bait*

Lamps dawdle in the field at midnight.
Three men follow their nose in the grass,
The lamp's beam their prow and compass.

The bucket's handle better not clatter now:
Silence and curious light gather bait.
Nab him, but wait

For the first shrinking, tacky on the thumb.
Let him re-settle backwards in his tunnel.
Then draw steady and he'll come.

Among the millions whorling their mud coronas
Under dew-lapped leaf and bowed blades,
A few are bound to be rustled in these night raids,

Innocent ventilators of the ground,
Making the globe a perfect fit,
A few are bound to be cheated of it

When lamps dawdle in the field at midnight,
When fishers need a garland for the bay
And have him, where he needs to come, out of the clay.

4. *Setting*

I

A line goes out of sight and out of mind
Down to the soft bottom of silt and sand
Past the indifferent skill of the hunting hand.

A bouquet of small hooks coiled in the stern
Is being paid out, back to its true form,
Until the bouquet's hidden in the worm.

The boat rides forward where the line slants back.
The oars in their locks go round and round.
The eel describes his arcs without a sound.

II

The gulls fly and umbrella overhead,
Treading air as soon as the line runs out,
Responsive acolytes above the boat.

Not sensible of any *kyrie*,
The fishers, who don't know and never try,
Pursue the work in hand as destiny.

They clear the bucket of the last chopped worms,
Pitching them high, good riddance, earthy shower.
The gulls encompass them before the water.

5. *Lifting*

They're busy in a high boat
That stalks towards Antrim, the power cut.
The line's a filament of smut

Drawn hand over fist
Where every three yards a hook's missed
Or taken (and the smut thickens, wrist-

Thick, a flail
Lashed into the barrel
With one swing). Each eel

Comes aboard to this welcome:
The hook left in gill or gum,
It's slapped into the barrel numb

But knits itself, four-ply,
With the furling, slippy
Haul, a knot of back and pewter belly

That stays continuously one
For each catch they fling in
Is sucked home like lubrication.

And wakes are enwound as the catch
On the morning water: which
Boat was which?

And when did this begin?
This morning, last year, when the lough first spawned?
The crews will answer, 'Once the season's in.'

6. *The Return*

In ponds, drains, dead canals,
she turns her head back,
older now, following
whim deliberately
till she's at sea in grass
and damned if she'll turn so
it's new trenches, sunk pipes,
swamps, running streams, the lough,
the river. Her stomach
shrunk, she exhilarates
in mid-water. Its throbbing
is speed through days and weeks.

Who knows now if she knows
her depth or direction?
She's passed Malin and
Tory, silent, wakeless,
a wisp, a wick that is
its own taper and light
through the weltering dark.
Where she's lost once she lays
ten thousand feet down in
her origins. The current
carries slicks of orphaned spawn.

7. *Vision*

Unless his hair was fine-combed,
The lice, they said, would gang up
Into a mealy rope
And drag him, small, dirty, doomed,

Down to the water. He was
Cautious then in riverbank
Fields. Thick as a birch trunk,
That cable flexed in the grass

Every time the wind passed. Years
Later in the same fields
He stood at night when eels
Moved through the grass like hatched fears

Towards the water. To stand
In one place as the field flowed
Past, a jellied road,
To watch the eels crossing land

Re-wound his world's live girdle.
Phosphorescent, sinewed slime
Continued at his feet. Time
Confirmed the horrid cable.

The Given Note

On the most westerly Blasket
In a dry-stone hut
He got this air out of the night.

Strange noises were heard
By others who followed, bits of a tune
Coming in on loud weather

Though nothing like melody.
He blamed their fingers and ear
As unpractised, their fiddling easy,

For he had gone alone into the island
And brought back the whole thing.
The house throbbed like his full violin.

So whether he calls it spirit music
Or not, I don't care. He took it
Out of wind off mid-Atlantic.

Still he maintains, from nowhere.
It comes off the bow gravely,
Rephrases itself into the air.

Whinlands

All year round the whin
Can show a blossom or two
But it's in full bloom now.
As if the small yolk stain

From all the birds' eggs in
All the nests of the spring
Were spiked and hung
Everywhere on bushes to ripen.

Hills oxidize gold.
Above the smoulder of green shoot
And dross of dead thorns underfoot
The blossoms scald.

Put a match under
Whins, they go up of a sudden.
They make no flame in the sun
But a fierce heat tremor

Yet incineration like that
Only takes the thorn –
The tough sticks don't burn,
Remain like bone, charred horn.

Gilt, jaggy, springy, frilled,
This stunted, dry richness
Persists on hills, near stone ditches,
Over flintbed and battlefield.

The Plantation

Any point in that wood
Was a centre, birch trunks
Ghosting your bearings,
Improvising charmed rings

Wherever you stopped.
Though you walked a straight line,
It might be a circle you travelled
With toadstools and stumps

Always repeating themselves.
Or did you re-pass them?
Here were bleyberries quilting the floor,
The black char of a fire,

And having found them once
You were sure to find them again.
Someone had always been there
Though always you were alone.

Lovers, birdwatchers,
Campers, gipsies and tramps
Left some trace of their trades
Or their excrement.

Hedging the road so,
It invited all comers
To the hush and the mush
Of its whispering treadmill,

Its limits defined,
So they thought, from outside.
They must have been thankful
For the hum of the traffic

If they ventured in
Past the picnickers' belt
Or began to recall
Tales of fog on the mountains.

You had to come back
To learn how to lose yourself,
To be pilot and stray – witch,
Hansel and Gretel in one.

Shoreline

Turning a corner, taking a hill
In County Down, there's the sea
Sidling and settling to
The back of a hedge. Or else

A grey foreshore with puddles
Dead-eyed as fish.
Haphazard tidal craters march
The corn and the grazing.

All round Antrim and westward
Two hundred miles at Moher
Basalt stands to.
Both ocean and channel

Froth at the black locks
On Ireland. And strands
Take hissing submissions
Off Wicklow and Mayo.

Take any minute. A tide
Is rummaging in
At the foot of all fields,
All cliffs and shingles.

Listen. Is it the Danes,
A black hawk bent on the sail?
Or the chinking Normans?
Or currachs hopping high

On to the sand?
Strangford, Arklow, Carrickfergus,
Belmullet and Ventry
Stay, forgotten like sentries.

Bann Clay

Labourers pedalling at ease
Past the end of the lane
Were white with it. Dungarees
And boots wore its powdery stain.

All day in open pits
They loaded on to the bank
Slabs like the squared-off clots
Of a blue cream. Sunk

For centuries under the grass,
It baked white in the sun,
Relieved its hoarded waters
And began to ripen.

It underruns the valley,
The first slow residue
Of a river finding its way.
Above it, the webbed marsh is new,

Even the clutch of Mesolithic
Flints. Once, cleaning a drain,
I shovelled up livery slicks
Till the water gradually ran

Clear on its old floor.
Under the humus and roots
This smooth weight. I labour
Towards it still. It holds and gluts.

Bogland

For T. P. Flanagan

We have no prairies
To slice a big sun at evening –
Everywhere the eye concedes to
Encroaching horizon,

Is wooed into the cyclops' eye
Of a tarn. Our unfenced country
Is bog that keeps crusting
Between the sights of the sun.

They've taken the skeleton
Of the Great Irish Elk
Out of the peat, set it up
An astounding crate full of air.

Butter sunk under
More than a hundred years
Was recovered salty and white.
The ground itself is kind, black butter

Melting and opening underfoot,
Missing its last definition
By millions of years.
They'll never dig coal here,

Only the waterlogged trunks
Of great firs, soft as pulp.
Our pioneers keep striking
Inwards and downwards,

Every layer they strip
Seems camped on before.
The bogholes might be Atlantic seepage.
The wet centre is bottomless.

Death of a Naturalist by SEAMUS HEANEY
First published in 1966. This edition published 2006.
Door into the Dark by SEAMUS HEANEY
First published in 1969. This edition published 2002.
This edition arranged with Faber and Faber Ltd. through Big Apple Agency, Inc.,
Labuan, Malaysia
Simplified Chinese edition copyright © 2024 Guangxi Normal University Press Group
Co., Ltd.

著作权合同登记号桂图登字:20 - 2024 - 003 号

图书在版编目(CIP)数据

一个博物学家之死;进入黑暗之门:中英双语版/(爱尔兰)
谢默斯·希尼著;朱玉译. —桂林:广西师范大学出版社,2024.5
(文学纪念碑)
书名原文:Death of a Naturalist/Door into the Dark
ISBN 978 - 7 - 5598 - 6850 - 3

Ⅰ.①一… Ⅱ.①谢… ②朱… Ⅲ.①诗集-爱尔兰-现代-
汉、英 Ⅳ.①I562.25

中国国家版本馆 CIP 数据核字(2024)第 061528 号

一个博物学家之死·进入黑暗之门:中英双语版
YIGE BOWUXUEJIA ZHI SI · JINRU HEIAN ZHI MEN: ZHONGYING SHUANGYU BAN

出 品 人:刘广汉   策 划:魏 东   责任编辑:魏 东 程卫平
助理编辑:钟雨晴   装帧设计:赵 瑾
广西师范大学出版社出版发行
(广西桂林市五里店路 9 号   邮政编码:541004)
网址:http://www.bbtpress.com
出版人:黄轩庄
全国新华书店经销
销售热线:021 - 65200318   021 - 31260822 - 898
山东临沂新华印刷物流集团有限责任公司印刷
(临沂高新技术产业开发区新华路 1 号   邮政编码:276017)
开本:889 mm×1 194 mm   1/32
印张:7.25   字数:214 千
2024 年 5 月第 1 版   2024 年 5 月第 1 次印刷
定价:66.00 元